Van stepped over the wall and into the circle

He stopped short, touched the butt of his pistol, then took off his hat, wiping at the sweat band.

"How do you want to do this?" he asked.

Fetterman laughed. "The easiest way possible. One of my men counts and we both draw on three."

"If I win, then your men will kill me."

"No, you go free. You'll have an hour's head start. But if my boys can find you, they'll cut you down."

"Fair enough. I'm ready," said Van.

Fetterman turned to one of his men. "Derek, you want to count this off?"

"Happy to," Kepler replied.

Fetterman reached down and unhooked the leather loop over the hammer of the stolen pistol. Then he looked at Billy the Zip, nodding to indicate that he was ready.

Van pushed back his hat slightly and licked his lips. He splayed his fingers, flexing them and then he, too, nodded.

"One," said Kepler, grinning broadly.

VIETNAM: GROUND ZERO™
GUNFIGHTER
ERIC HELM

A GOLD EAGLE BOOK FROM
WORLDWIDE®

TORONTO · NEW YORK · LONDON · PARIS
AMSTERDAM · STOCKHOLM · HAMBURG
ATHENS · MILAN · TOKYO · SYDNEY

First edition February 1990

ISBN 0-373-62722-X

VIETNAM: GROUND ZERO.

GUNFIGHTER

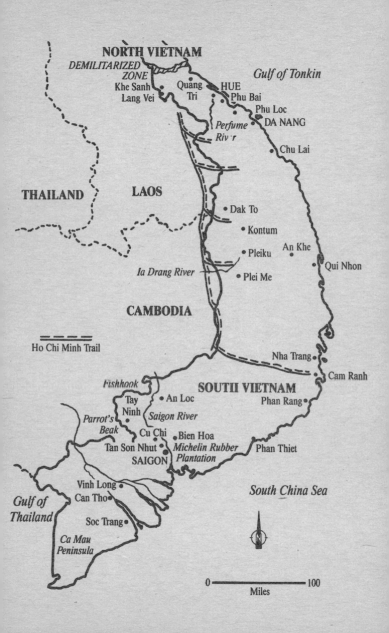

PROLOGUE

JUNGLES NEAR THUAN LOI REPUBLIC OF VIETNAM

The prisoner-of-war camp was nestled in the mountains, protected by triple-canopy jungle and a single high cliff. Mud-and-thatch huts were pushed back against the huge, smooth-trunked teak trees. From some of the trees, thick bamboo cages dangled five or six feet off the ground. A single, long, low building with a split-log floor served as a barracks for the guards. Near it was a smaller hut that doubled as a barracks for the officers and headquarters for the commander.

It was a small camp, tucked in among the trees and bushes. A single path, carved out of the jungle in order to make it invisible from the air, led up to the camp. At the center of the military base was a circular area almost thirty feet in diameter. The cleared area was contained by a short rock wall no more than two feet high. To the north were bleachers, which lent the circle the appearance of an outdoor lecture hall.

NVA Captain Nguyen Vo Van sat in the tiny headquarters building near its single window and used a small pistol cleaning rod to scour the barrel of his Colt single-shot revolver. He'd bought it seven years ago while attending school at the University of California at Berkeley on a grant from the American government. He'd only been there for a semester, and then the hostilities between North Vietnam and the United States had escalated, forcing him to leave school. But in those few months he'd learned to love the western as a legitimate form of literature. He might not have learned much about the United States or Western culture, but he did learn to love cowboy movies.

Van was a small man, just over five feet. He weighed almost a hundred pounds, had brown eyes and long jet-black hair, which he wore in a ponytail to mimic some of the photos he'd seen of real American cowboys. His round face was marked by broad, flat features. A scar ran from his chin, up his left cheek and then to his ear, the top of which was missing.

When he heard a knock on the door, Van looked up. Sergeant Tuyen Tri Tran stood there. Taller and heavier than Van, Tran's black hair was cut quite short on the sides of his head but left longer on top. His features were pushed together at the center of his face, and his skin was badly scarred by smallpox. He wasn't a pretty sight, but good looks mattered very little to him, anyway.

"Everything is ready," Tran said in Vietnamese, bowing slightly as he entered the room.

"You have spoken to the American and he's agreed?" asked Van.

"Of course, Comrade. What choice does he have? Either a gunfight with you or a hanging."

Van nodded and set his weapon on a wobbly wooden table. "But he does understand he has a real choice, doesn't he?"

"Yes, he understands."

"Good."

"The men are assembling," said Tran. "The bleachers will be filled in five minutes."

Van stood and moved to the rear of the building, passing through a doorway. There was a cot against one wall, a small stand with a drawer in it and a trunk. Van knelt in front of the trunk and took out one of the three western shirts he owned. This one had mother-of-pearl snaps and a white fringe. The trunk also contained blue jeans and cowboy boots.

Slowly Van dressed. Then he took his hand-tooled leather holster from the trunk. It had been made on his return to Vietnam. Finally he donned his cowboy hat, positioning it carefully on his head, tilting it just so. Then, fully dressed, with his holster tied down low, he moved back through the doorway. At the window he could see the center circle, the bleachers and the American soldier, who was young and wore torn, dirty jungle fatigues and scuffed, almost gray jungle boots.

The American wore a holster, also tied down low, but he had no pistol. He stood, facing west, his shoulders sloped. He looked tired and frightened and ready to run, if he thought he could get away.

"It's time," said Van, grinning. "Time to teach the imperialist a lesson." He picked up his pistol and slowly loaded it. Holding the hammer back with his thumb and the trigger down with his index finger, he gave the cylinder a spin, just as he'd seen John Wayne do in a dozen movies. "I'm ready."

Tran left the office and descended the wooden steps to the narrow porch. Van walked out behind him and stopped for a moment, one hand on his hip, the other on the butt of the pistol stuck into his holster. He took a deep breath, but rather than smelling the dry, hot air of the American Southwest, he felt the heat and humidity of Southeast Asia.

The leather of his boots scraped on the wooden planks of the porch. Van stepped off into the dirt of the makeshift street. He put a hand to his forehead just under the brim of his hat, then walked to the circle where the American waited.

Stepping over the low stone wall, he faced the American soldier. Van knew the man was tired. The GI hadn't slept much the night before, thanks to a Co Cong. She'd spent the night with the American as a reward for his bravery in facing Van's gun. Although the man hadn't been well fed in the past three weeks, he'd been given as much as he could eat in the past two days.

Van stood flat-footed, hands on his hips, and stared into the eyes of the American soldier. The man's hard blue eyes seemed to hold no fear now.

"Are you ready?" asked Van.

"I kill you and they'll kill me," the man said, nodding at the soldiers in the bleachers.

"You kill me," said Van, "and you're free to leave this camp. You'll have to make your own way back to one of your bases, but my men won't interfere."

"I haven't got a weapon."

Van pointed at Tran and snapped his fingers. Tran handed a pistol to the American—a Smith and Wesson .38 with a four-inch barrel. The man took it and looked at it.

"You have only two bullets," Van said. "If you try anything funny, you'll be shot immediately. If you cheat, you'll die."

The man shoved the pistol into the holster, stood for a moment, then grabbed at it. He adjusted his belt so that the butt of the pistol was at palm-level, with his arm hanging straight down. He could draw more easily that way.

"If you're ready," said Van.

"Go."

"The rules are simple. We face each other, and one of my men counts to three. On three we draw and fire. You have two shots to kill me."

"And you have six."

"I've never needed more than one," Van said. "If you win, you can go. If you lose, we'll bury you in the jungle so that you'll be of some use to us by fertilizing the ground."

"Enough talking," said the American.

Van reached down and unhooked the leather thong knotted over the hammer of his pistol. He wiped a hand on his chest, then nodded, indicating that he, too, was ready. Turning his attention toward the American, he waited for the countdown to begin.

Tran looked at Van, at the American, then back at Van. "One," he said finally.

The American flexed his fingers and stared at Van. He watched his adversary's eyes and waited.

"Two."

Van drew then, his gun slipping from the holster smoothly. As he drew, he thumbed back the hammer and raised the weapon.

The American grabbed at his own revolver. He dropped to one knee as he drew, clearing the holster as Van fired. The round missed, snapping by his head. He dived to the left, rolled and aimed at the Vietnamese officer.

Van stood calmly, his right side toward the American, his pistol straight out in front of him as he aimed. There was a second shot. The bullet took the American in the shoulder with a loud, wet impact. The GI groaned out loud and fired a bullet into the dirt.

Van fired a third time. The bullet slammed into the American's head. A small, dark, third eye appeared as the back of his head bulged and then blew out in a spray of blood and brain. He spasmed, the kick flipping him over onto his back. His feet drummed the soft dirt of the circle while one hand clawed at the ground.

Van stood still, his pistol aimed at the dying man. He waited until the ground was soaked crimson and the spasms subsided. It was quiet then, the Vietnamese in the bleachers strangely silent as the first of the jungle flies dived at the blood.

Then, suddenly, there was a burst of applause followed by wild cheering. Van grinned at his soldiers and bowed. He held his weapon high for them to admire, then turned toward Tran and said, "Have the garbage removed."

As the men continued to cheer, Van turned and walked back to his headquarters. He climbed the steps to the porch and entered the building. Sitting down at the table, he took out his combat knife and carefully cut another notch into the handle of his pistol. It joined the twenty others he'd put there in the past six months. Twenty men had died in that circle. Twenty men who'd thought they were being given a chance to escape. Twenty men who had died so that Van could build his reputation as the fastest gun in Southeast Asia.

Before any of his men came to see him, Van reloaded his pistol, replacing the two spent cartridges. Then, moving to his trunk, he took out a bottle of American bourbon and drank from it. He'd seen that in the movies, too. The winner always took a drink after a fight to celebrate victory. Or to calm his nerves.

Tran knocked on the door, leaned in and said, "The men would like you to make another appearance. A chance to see their commanding officer."

Van nodded and stood up. Who was he to deny the men a chance to see their hero? He joined Tran and walked back to the circle, listening to the cheering of his men.

1

MACV HEADQUARTERS
SAIGON

Special Forces Captain MacKenzie K. Gerber sat in the vinyl visitor's chair that had been patched with black electrician's tape and thought about all the other things he could be doing at that moment. Robin Morrow, a reporter, was still in Saigon, and she had invited Gerber to stay with her. They, along with Master Sergeant Anthony B. Fetterman, could be checking out the activity on Tu Do Street, eating at the poshest restaurant at the Carasel or drinking in the rooftop garden. There were things to be done, none of which included hanging around with the local CIA spook.

Instead, Gerber, along with Fetterman, was sitting in the basement office of Jerry Maxwell, a civilian who worked for the CIA. The walls of Maxwell's office were made of cinder block that had been recently painted light blue. The room contained a desk, a visitor's chair and a bank of filing cabinets. The floor was covered in worn dirty green tile.

Gerber and Fetterman, nearly unconscious because of the monotone briefing, listened to Maxwell drone on and on about the latest hot project the CIA had come up with. The CIA agent was nearly lost behind his desk, which was piled high with reports, documents and empty Coke cans.

Maxwell, a short, skinny man, was dressed in a white suit with a white shirt and a narrow black tie, just as he always was. He had loosened his collar and pulled the tie down. His suit coat was draped over the back of his chair. In the past few months Maxwell's hair had started to fall out in clumps. This had frightened him at first but, as he was brushing his teeth one day, he had looked at the top of his head and realized that he didn't care if all his hair fell out. Having a full head of hair wasn't one of the priorities in his life. Living through the tour in Vietnam was one. Moving up in the CIA was one. But having all his hair wasn't.

Picking up a folder and then waving it as if it were a banner, Maxwell said, "I've been handed a real problem here. A sticky problem."

Fetterman, who was leaning against the filing cabinets in the corner, said, "And now it's going to be our problem."

Fetterman was a diminutive man. He'd lost a good deal of his black hair, and his deep tropical tan gave him an almost Latin look. The thickness of his beard, which required him to shave twice a day, merely added to that impression. He had a nondescript look, almost like a door-to-door salesman, but he was one of the most deadly men alive. He understood warfare, he understood the jungle and he understood the enemy. And anyone who looked into his eyes would understand that. He had gray-black eyes that were as hard as coal and as deep as a bottomless pit. Anyone who examined those killer eyes knew not to cross Fetterman. Ever.

The master sergeant glanced idly at the top of the filing cabinets. They, like Maxwell's desk, were covered with a blizzard of paper. There were files, reports and documents, all of them unclassified, but all relating to the war in some fashion. The last cabinet was a bulky thing with a combination lock on the second drawer.

Maxwell pushed the file folder toward Gerber, then said to Fetterman, "It's everyone's problem. Everyone who's fighting in South Vietnam."

Gerber took the folder and opened it. Gerber was a tall, young man who had barely passed thirty. He had fair hair, bleached by the sun, a deep tropical tan and a slender frame.

"Report there," said Maxwell, "is about a North Vietnamese called Billy the Zip."

"Billy the Zip?" Gerber queried.

Maxwell laughed. "That's the name he's been given. The rumors we have... maybe I should say the Intelligence reports we have, indicate that old Billy is staging gunfights."

"What in hell are you talking about?" asked Gerber. He shot a glance at Fetterman.

Maxwell held up a hand. "Let me start at the beginning. During the last, oh, three, four months, we've heard stories of a North Vietnamese officer challenging POWs to gunfights. Old West-style gunfights. Two men facing each other down, drawing and firing with one man ending up dead."

"Jesus," said Gerber, whistling.

"Billy always wins," Maxwell continued. "He's fast and he's good. According to our information, only one man has ever gotten a shot off against him, and that was a bullet into the dirt. No one has come close to killing Billy the Zip."

"And what's this got to do with Sergeant Fetterman and me?" Gerber asked, already knowing the answer.

"Stories of Billy are circulating throughout Three Corps, and we're afraid it's going to affect morale."

"You mean there are men who'll actually believe this bullshit?" asked Fetterman.

"It's true," Maxwell replied. "We know it's true. Billy has started bragging about it."

"Now, how do you know that?" asked Gerber.

"We're not totally without sources," said Maxwell. "Billy or his soldiers talk about it in a village, and the Vietnamese working for us overhear it and report it."

"And you believe it?" Gerber asked.

"Well, naturally, we rate it according to the source. But we've gotten the story from more than one source, and each time the story surfaces, it's that much more believable."

"Have you got any evidence?" Fetterman probed.

Maxwell hesitated, then nodded. "The last few bodies have been dumped close to large base camps. The latest was found just outside of Dau Tieng. An American soldier shot twice. The man was identified as a soldier missing in action. All this is, of course, in violation of the Geneva Convention."

"I wasn't aware that North Vietnam had signed the agreement," said Gerber.

Maxwell shrugged. "It violates the rules of land warfare, then. It's a crime against humanity."

Gerber shook his head. "Save the speeches. Do our men get a loaded weapon?"

"Rumors are that each man was supplied with a loaded handgun. One or two rounds is all, but they did have a fair chance."

"That's something," said Fetterman. "What is our response going to be?"

"I thought that maybe you two—"

"No," snapped Fetterman. "What's our official response? Aren't we filling the diplomatic channels with protests?"

"No," Maxwell said. "The feeling is that such a move would only invite press interest, and we're afraid that Billy would increase his activities if his name began appearing in the papers."

"What you're really saying is that nothing has been done about this," Gerber said.

Maxwell picked up one of the empty Coke cans and shook it. Finding nothing in it, he set it down, then said, "The feeling was that the aberration would take care of itself. Billy would be reined in by his superiors, especially when he began to shoot off his mouth in the local villages, but no one has done a thing about it."

"So you're handing this to us?" asked Gerber.

"I was hoping you'd look at the problem and come up with a solution."

Gerber tapped the file folder with his index finger. "Where is this Billy's camp?"

"Three Corps," Maxwell answered. "Northern end of Three Corps in the mountains there."

"That certainly limits the area we'd have to search," Fetterman said sarcastically. "Down to a couple of hundred square miles."

"Well, you can use the men at the Special Forces camp at Song Be to help. Twenty-fifth Infantry from Tay Ninh and Dau Tieng are also interested in the problem, as is the First Air Cav."

"Seems to be a poorly planned project," Gerber said. "One with little chance of success."

"Look," Maxwell conceded, "I won't try to fool you two. You know the score. Right now we've only gotten some rumors about this and the location of Billy's camp, and that's all we've got. You'll have to organize the whole thing. I'll give you everything we know, but that isn't much."

Gerber took a deep breath. "Jerry, this isn't something we should be doing."

"Why not? Both of you are the perfect people for this. If anyone can locate Billy, it's Fetterman. Then you just swoop in, eliminate the camp and kill Billy. You'll be freeing the POWs in the camp, as well."

"Regular leg outfits could do it," Fetterman argued.

"Tony, you know better than that. Regular legs are good at search-and-destroy and attacking known enemy positions, but this one calls for finesse. The kind of expertise that you and Captain Gerber have."

"We're sunk," said Fetterman. "He starts laying it on this thick and we're sunk."

Gerber handed the folder back to Maxwell. "I'll tell you what we'll do. We'll look into this and see what we can learn. If we come up with anything concrete, then maybe we can design a plan that'll work. If not, we're not going to waste a lot of our time."

"I can't ask for more," said Maxwell.

"The hell you couldn't," Gerber replied. "The hell you couldn't."

THEY HAD BEEN IN THE FIELD since sunup. The helicopters had landed as the sun had begun to peek over the horizon, and the men had scrambled onto them. They'd then ridden toward the jungles north of Dau Tieng. No one had spoken. The noise of the Huey's engines and the popping of the rotors had made conversation difficult.

Besides, most of the men were still tired from the beer party hosted by the company commander the night before. He'd received his orders for home and had ordered a half-dozen cases of beer flown in for the men to help him celebrate his survival of his year in Vietnam.

Spec Four Harrison Williams only drank one of the beers. Williams was a young man, only nineteen, and had yet to acquire a taste for beer. But because he was a member of the company, and because Captain Davis had bought the beer, he felt obligated to drink it, even if he didn't want it.

When he finished his beer, he sat on low wall of sandbags and listened to the rock music coming from a tape player. The Stones, the Beatles and a dozen other groups played late into the night while another company guarded the perimeter.

As the last of the music died, Williams stood and walked across the red dust of the compound to the low hootch that he shared with a dozen other men. There were cots lining the walls, footlockers at the end of the beds and wall lockers standing between each position. A community radio set sat on a small table constructed from cannibalized ammo boxes. Someone had bought a TV, but AFVN-TV wasn't on the air and wouldn't be until the next afternoon.

Williams collapsed onto his cot after taking off his jungle shirt. He kept his pants and boots on because the enemy often dropped a few mortar rounds or a couple of rockets during the night. The mortar shells and rockets rarely did any damage and rarely wounded anyone, but when they started falling no one wanted to hang around searching for boots. More than once a man had dived into a bunker naked, his feet cut up from running across open ground.

Although it seemed that only an hour had passed, it was actually closer to five. Williams came awake suddenly, alert, aware of the man standing in the doorway telling them all that it was time to get up. As the door closed, one of the men lit a Coleman lantern so that they could see. Grumbling, they all dressed for a day in the field—clean uniform, new socks and old boots. Each man had three canteens, some of the squad equipment and enough ammo to keep him in a firefight at full-auto for a long time. If they needed anything else, it would be brought in by chopper during the day.

They all ate a cold breakfast and drank as much juice and water as possible because the day would be hot. Then they walked out to the landing strip. Groups of six or seven men, dressed in baggy fatigues, carried M-16s, M-60s and M-79s. They were young men, high school refugees under the command of officers who themselves were barely out of college.

"Christ," said Bill Divies, "I shouldn't have drunk that last beer. Fucking head feels like it's goin' to explode. Christ."

"Don't get sick on me," said Williams. "Do it in the seeds over there."

"I ain't gonna throw up. That's a waste of good alcohol. Didn't eat no breakfast, so there's no reason to be throwing up anywhere."

Williams sat down, holding his rifle in both hands between his knees. He wanted to say something, but everything sounded like a bad line from a war movie. In fact, he, along with Divies, Tomás Chavez and Jimmy Littleton, had sat around one night talking as if they were in a movie. They had talked about the war and home and how, if they were in a movie, each of them would require a name that reflected his civilian occupation, except that none of them had a civilian occupation. They'd all made it into the Army before any of them had had the chance to learn a civilian occupation. There was no Preacher, Professor or Shyster. They were a bunch of high school kids who belonged at home trying to figure out a way to stay out all night.

Sergeant Martin walked over. A tall, heavy man, he wore a clean uniform and carried a CAR-15. He was an imposing man who shaved his head, including his eyebrows, which gave him a menacing look. He stopped, looked down at Williams and ordered, "On your feet."

"Chopper's not here."

"They're inbound," said Martin. "So just get on your feet and don't give me a ration of shit about it."

"Yes, sir, Sergeant, sir." Williams stood and brushed the dust from his pants.

"And knock off the smart talk," Martin warned as he walked off toward the second load.

The lift went off easily. The choppers landed in swirling dust and grass, loaded, then took off in more clouds of dust, flying toward the LZ selected by the command staff the night before. The target was a small section of triple-canopy jungle where they hadn't been for a month. They touched down in a large clearing ringed by bunkers that had been abandoned. There was no sign that Charlie had been there in weeks.

They'd swept the bunker line, tearing it up as much as they could, caving in the tops of bunkers and ripping out the logs set in them. Williams had wished they'd brought their entrenching tools to tear up the bunkers. It would have been easier than using knifes and bayonets or bare hands.

Now they were deep in the jungle. The undergrowth was thick and tore at their uniforms, trying to hold them back. The heat and humidity hung in the air almost visibly. It was like walking through a steam bath wrapped in a hot towel. Sweat soaked their uniforms, turning them black. There was no relief from the heat. No breeze blew through the jungle. Nothing.

The pace slowed as the men fought with the jungle. Birds squawked and monkeys screamed. Insects, attracted by the men's sweat, darted at their eyes and buzzed around their ears. The soldiers tried to ignore them, occasionally waving a hand to chase them away.

At noon they halted and fanned out in a rough circle, half the men watching while the other half ate a cold meal of C-rats. After thirty minutes they changed roles. The meal finished, the company commander, Captain Davis, divided them into platoons, giving each of the lieutenants a specific area to search with everyone rendezvousing an hour before dusk for extraction by the helicopters. They could cover more ground that way and still be out before dark.

Williams and his platoon, commanded by Lieutenant Ralph Klein, moved off to the south down a slight slope to a narrow valley with a creek at the bottom. The ground turned marshy, spongy and wet. All the men moved carefully, trying to stay out of the water until, one by one, they somehow got wet and no longer cared. The tepid water rose above their knees in places, filling their boots. They splashed through it, found drier ground on the other side and began a slow climb to the top of another rise.

When they finally reached it, the men dropped to the ground to rest. Klein tried to set up security, but the exertion of the walk through the marshy ground and the climb to the top of the ridge had sapped their strength. Halfheartedly they watched the jungle around them, searching for the enemy they had yet to see. Only the birds and animals seemed to have any energy, and they seemed to be moving in slow motion, too.

After a twenty-minute break, during which the men drank most of the water they carried with them, Sergeant Martin urged them to their feet. They then began the task of walking along the ridge line, not worried about being on the top. With the jungle all around them, some of the trees over two hundred feet tall, they weren't afraid of being silhouetted against the bright blue sky.

The burst of machine gun fire caught them off guard. Martin dived for the trunk of a teak tree, trying to roll between the roots that stuck up like the fingers of an arthritic hand. He popped up once, fired, then dropped down. As he rose to fire again, a bullet smashed into his forehead just under the rim of his steel pot. He collapsed, blood spurting, a hand clawing at the air.

The rest of the men scattered and returned fire. Williams crouched behind a bush, his left shoulder against a palm trunk.

"Fire!" screamed Lieutenant Klein. "Open fire! *Open fire!*"

There was an explosion, a dull pop as a Chicom grenade detonated. Shrapnel whistled through the air. Rounds snapped overhead, stripping bark from the trees. Bits of wood and leaf rained down.

"Take them on the right. On the right!" yelled Divies.

"There, by the tree. Get that guy," someone called out.

"Medic! I need a medic! Please," another man pleaded.

Klein dived to the right, where the RTO lay face-down on the jungle floor. He scrambled forward, keeping low. The odor of rotting vegetation filled his nostrils, but he took little notice of it.

Reaching the RTO's body, he could see the man was dead. Part of his head had been blown away, revealing the brain. The lieutenant snagged the handset from the hand of the dead man. Through it he could hear the carrier wave loud and clear. Squeezing the button, he yelled, "Apache Six, Apache Six, this is Apache Three-six."

"Go, Three-six."

"We are—" A burst of machine gun fire rocked the body of the dead RTO. Bullets slammed into the radio with dull, quiet snaps. The handset was jerked from the lieutenant's grasp as the radio died. He scrambled after it, jammed it up to his mouth and shouted, "I have a fire mission, over." But there was no response and no carrier wave.

Tossing away the useless handset, the lieutenant whirled, lifted his M-16 and fired at the muzzle-flashes, bright in the trees. He flipped the selector switch to full-auto and held the trigger down. Growling deep in his throat, he hosed down the jungle. When the weapon was empty, he yanked the magazine from it and tossed it away, trying to get to a fresh one.

The first round hit him in the shoulder, flipping him backward. He still tried to reload, aware of the pain in his shoulder and the wetness spreading over his chest. He tried to sit up so that he could open fire, but a second round caught him in the stomach, punching through his back. He slipped down, pain blazing in his belly. There was firing all around him. A hundred weapons—AKs and M-16s—hammered at one another, and they confused him completely. He died, wondering what was happening.

More of the platoon was killed. Some of them were caught in a cross fire that ripped them apart. A few were felled by shrapnel from the grenades. One man was hit in the arm just as he jerked a pin from a grenade. He dropped it at his own feet. Then, blinded by the pain, he couldn't find it again. It exploded, killing him instantly.

Williams slipped deeper into the jungle, his back against a thick tree trunk. He emptied his weapon, dropped the spent magazine onto the jungle floor and reloaded. Searching the jungle around him, he spotted the muzzle-flashes of an AK. He put a burst into it and saw the enemy soldier fall. Williams screamed like a Rebel soldier hitting the Union line at Gettysburg.

Spinning to his left, he fired into the jungle again. But as he did, he noticed that the number of M-16s had been reduced. The hammering of the weapons had faded slightly. Now he could hear the detonations of individual weapons. His friends were dying quickly.

A man appeared to his right, rising up from the gloom of the jungle floor. Whirling, Williams fired once, twice, and the VC dropped again.

Williams fell back against the trunk of the tree. Sweat dripped from his face. His hands were slick with it. His belly was ice-cold. There weren't many M-16s firing now. Most of his friends were dead.

Williams emptied his weapon again, reloaded and continued to shoot. As he ran out of ammo, a man came running at him, head down. Williams jerked his combat knife from the scabbard and stood to meet the threat. He turned as the man attacked, slashing with his blade. The VC screamed as the knife sliced through his arm. He whirled, aiming at Williams, who stepped closer, grabbing the barrel of the AK. He plunged the knife into the man's chest.

The VC collapsed, falling onto his back, his hands on Williams's arm, pulling at him. Williams leaned in, trying to shove the knife through the man's body. He twisted it, his shoulder lowered and his teeth bared. The man kicked out once and blood bubbled from his open mouth. He coughed up a pink froth. Then, suddenly, the man's hands fell away and his eyes glazed over.

Rocking back, Williams pulled at his knife, ripping it from the dead man. As it came free, he realized that there was no more firing. The jungle was quiet, except for the groans of the wounded. At that moment he looked up into the barrel of an AK-47 and into the grinning face of a Vietcong soldier.

2

CARASEL HOTEL
SAIGON

Gerber stood at the bar, leaning on it, waiting for someone to take his order. Taped rock music blared out, shaking the building with its driving beat. There was a babble of conversation, but it was all but drowned out by the music. It was an almost impossible place in which to talk, let alone spy in. No one could overhear a conversation without it being obvious they were trying to overhear.

The bartender arrived and leaned close to Gerber. The young Vietnamese man grinned at the captain with broken yellow teeth and yelled, "You want?"

"Three beers!" shouted Gerber in response. With the noise as loud as it was, he figured he'd be lucky to get even one.

But the man returned with three glasses and three bottles. Moisture was beaded on the outside, indicating they had been cold once. Gerber dropped his MPCs on the bar and picked up the tray with the glasses and beer. When he reached the table, Fetterman stood up and yelled, "We'll never be able to talk in here."

Gerber glanced at Morrow and then at the master sergeant. Morrow was easier to look at. She was a tall, slender woman who, like everyone else in Vietnam, was beginning to look like a prisoner of war on bread and water. There were fatigue circles under her eyes, as if she had been slugged. Still, she was a good-looking woman with long hair bleached blond by the sun.

"So, who wants to talk?" asked Gerber.

"I thought that was the point of this exercise," said Fetterman. "Quiz Miss Morrow."

She turned her attention to Fetterman. "I like that. Every time he wants something, I revert to Miss Morrow. Why is that, Master Sergeant?"

"Hell," said Fetterman, shrugging, "I don't know."

"Good answer," Morrow chided. Gerber set the beers in front of each of them and then handed out the glasses. Morrow poured beer slowly into her glass, then took a sip. Over the music she shouted, "One thing that being in Vietnam has taught me and that's to drink beer. Couldn't stand the stuff before I got here. Couldn't even stand the thought of the stuff."

Fetterman nodded. "And sometimes it's the only cold drink available."

Gerber lifted his glass in a toast, couldn't think of anything profound, then finally said, "To a short war and a long career."

They drank and then Morrow leaned close to Gerber. "What is it that you and Tony would like to know?"

Gerber glanced at the rooftop garden. There was enough vegetation in the pots and hanging planters to make it look like a jungle. A bar was set off to one side, and there was a small area for dancing, though in the heat of the afternoon no one was interested in moving around much. There was also a great view of downtown Saigon, but no one seemed interested in looking at downtown Saigon. No one ever felt like doing that.

Gerber sipped his beer and finally asked, "Have you heard anything about the Vietcong?"

Morrow laughed. "I've heard lots of things about the Vietcong. What did you have in mind?"

The music died for a moment, and then the speakers seemed to explode. The rooftop was filled with sound as one of the Rolling Stones began to scream.

"That tears it," said Fetterman. "I can't hear a fucking thing."

Gerber shrugged. "Let's get off the roof. It's too hot out here, anyway. I never could figure out the advantage of sitting in a simulated jungle that's elevated so that it's closer to the sun."

Fetterman picked up his glass and then his bottle. "I'm not unhappy about returning to the air-conditioning and the quiet inside."

"Go," Morrow said.

They walked through the French doors, descended the three steps that led down to the floor and found a table on the opposite side of the room. They wanted to be as far from the French doors as they could get.

After they sat down, Gerber took a drink. "I've got to try to get some information from you without giving you much in return."

"Thank you very much," Morrow replied.

"But in asking the questions, I could give away more than I want, so the questions are going to be, well, strange. Very strange."

Morrow leaned back in her chair and stared. "Stranger than the last one?"

"I'm afraid so." Gerber looked around the room. There were Vietnamese men and women carrying drinks and food to the American military officers who had ordered them. There were also a few South Vietnamese officials and military officers scattered around the room. But no one was close to them.

"Well?" asked Morrow.

Gerber shrugged. "The first question stands. Have you heard any strange stories about the Vietcong or their officers lately?"

"You mean like they looked over all the camps prior to the Tet attacks?"

"Something like that," said Gerber, nodding. He knew that before Tet the VC and NVA officers who would be leading assaults had toured each of the bases using faked or stolen identity papers. Treaty requirements demanded that the South Vietnamese have access to all areas of American bases with the exception of the most critical zones, such as the flight lines.

For a moment Morrow sat quietly, her eyes closed in thought. Finally she opened her eyes, looked at Gerber and shook her head. "Nothing."

"Robin, have you heard any stories about any individuals, VC or NVA, who are, shall we say, flamboyant?"

"There was a story about some fighter pilot up north who thinks of himself as the number one ace in the entire world. The North Vietnamese propaganda machine has done something with him. Stories in the Eastern Bloc press. An Order of Lenin or something like that."

"Nope," said Gerber. "That's not it."

"Well, it would help a great deal if you could tell me what you're looking for."

Gerber drained his beer. "I'm sure it would, but I can't tell you any more. We're trying not to taint the information by asking leading questions."

"Then there isn't much I can do for you." She looked directly at Gerber. "In that respect."

"My goodness," said Fetterman, looking at his watch in mock surprise. "Is it three o'clock already? I'd better be going, or I'm going to be late."

"Oh, stuff it, Fetterman," snapped Gerber.

"Yes, sir."

Morrow glanced at her watch. "I really should put in an appearance at the office, even if it's only to tell them I don't know anything new."

"How about dinner tonight?" asked Gerber.

"Oh, I'm counting on that." She stood and asked, "Is it my turn to buy a round?"

"No," said Gerber. "That's not necessary. What time will you be ready?"

"Six. Six-thirty."

"I'll see you then," said Gerber.

She started to walk away, then turned back and leaned forward with one hand on the table so that he could see down the top of her jumpsuit. "You want my help on this, you'll have to give me more to go on."

"Robin, right now there's no more to go on. It was an idle question spawned by something we overheard this morning. That's all."

"Sure. Well, I'll see you for dinner." She turned and walked off.

Gerber watched her go, thinking that even the modified jumpsuit she wore looked good on her.

"You think she bought that?" Fetterman asked.

"Hell, no," said Gerber. "She's not stupid."

"Think she'll come up with anything to help us?"

"Nope."

WHEN THE FIRING died away and his soldiers had captured the American who had survived, Captain Van stepped out of hiding. He wore a dark green uniform with no insignia on it. As usual, his cowboy gun belt was slung low. He moved to the captured American, who was kneeling over the body of the dead VC soldier, waiting for the hammer to fall.

One of his men came up to him. "Comrade, there are wounded."

Van looked at the American and then at his soldier. "Where are they?"

"Follow me."

Moving among the American bodies scattered over the jungle floor, they passed the platoon leader, Lieutenant Davis, who lay near the riddled RTO. Both were obviously dead from multiple wounds. Blood had pooled under them, the flies already gathering in the wounds. The black, buzzing mass shifted and surged, making it look as if the skin were still alive, even though the men were dead.

They came to another body. Blood stained the uniform, and a hand was missing. White bone showed through, looking moist, as if covered with water. Van knelt and looked into the face of the dead man. If it hadn't been for the missing hand and the blood on his back, he would have looked as if he had fallen asleep in the jungle. Van touched the man's throat, but there was no pulse.

"Over here," said one of his men. He pointed at a man lying facedown on the trail. Blood stained the ground near him. The back of the soldier was moving, as if he were breathing rapidly.

Van stepped up to the man and looked down at him. There was a bullet hole in the GI's back, just under his shoulder blade. Another bullet had gone through his left buttock, a third through his right hand. The man's eyes were closed, and his face was pasty white.

Van drew his pistol, thumbed the hammer back and aimed at the man's head. He grinned, glanced at the men around him, then pulled the trigger. The round slammed into the back of the man's head and blew out the front. The American's body went rigid as he died.

"Another over here," someone called out.

Van turned and stared. The next American was lying on his side, but he was conscious. Van moved toward him and then asked the soldier guarding him, "Is he badly wounded?"

"Bullet through both legs. He can't walk."

Again Van cocked his pistol and aimed.

"Hey, man," said the American. "You can't do that. It's against the rules."

Van smiled, then said in English, "The rules are what I make them."

"Hey, man," said the American again. Now his voice was tinged with fear, but he stared up at Van.

Van didn't respond. Instead, he fired at the man's head, blowing the back out. The dead man spasmed once and then was still.

"Comrade," Tran said, "it's time for us to get out of here."

"Wait," said another soldier. "We've got another wounded American."

Van followed the man to where the wounded American sat. His head was down and he held a bloodied bandage against his shoulder. He looked up, stared at Van, then asked in a voice furred by pain, "You going to murder me, too?"

"Can you walk?" Van enquired.

"I can walk."

"Then you have just saved your own life. Get to your feet. You fall down, you slow us down, and you'll die immediately with no right to appeal to a higher authority. Keep up with us and you'll live."

The American stood slowly. He wavered for a moment, looked as if he were about to collapse, then steadied himself. Wiping a hand over his forehead, he said defiantly, "Anytime."

Van pointed at Tran and ordered, "Strip everything of value from the dead. Everything."

"Yes, Comrade."

"Bring the prisoner," said Van. He whirled and headed back to the other American, who was waiting. Van looked at him. "You're lucky."

"I saw," said the man.

"Help your friend, or I'll be forced to shoot him. We won't be slowed down by him."

"Of course." He moved to where the wounded man stood and took his arm, helping him stand.

"Shit," said the man. "We're in trouble."

"We're okay now. If you can stay on your feet, you'll be okay."

"I don't know, man. I don't feel so good."

"You've got to try."

"Shut up," Van said. "There'll be no talking, or I'll shoot both of you now."

"I knew I should have shot myself in the foot last week," muttered the wounded man. "I knew it."

Neither man watched as the VC stripped the bodies, taking everything from them. The victors took watches, wallets and military equipment. They took clothes that weren't blood-soaked and equipment that hadn't been damaged in the fighting. They left broken equipment and damaged rifles and ignored the radio, which had been filled with bullet holes.

Finally they finished, and Van moved to where the prisoners waited. "We go now. If you give us any trouble, you'll both be shot."

The two prisoners nodded glumly.

"Then we go."

Van waited as two of his men ran off into the jungle, heading toward their camp. A moment after they disappeared, the whole unit began to move. Slowly. They stayed off the paths and in the deep jungle to avoid American helicopters and fighters crisscrossing the sky. They moved slowly, each man being overly careful, avoiding damaging the plants and trying not to disturb the rotting vegetation on the jungle floor. It was of paramount importance that they leave no trail from the ambush site. That was what protected them. Such precautions ensured that the Americans would be unable to find their camp.

Van wasn't in a hurry. He knew that the Americans weren't following. He knew that it would be days before the Americans found the ambush site and that they would busy themselves with getting the bodies out once they'd located them. No one would be that interested in following his men, even if they could find the trail.

It had been a good ambush. It had resulted in a great deal of new equipment, new ammo and two new contestants in Van's wild West gunfights. And, for Billy the Zip, that had been the real reason for the mission.

3

MACV-SOG TAN SON
NHUT SAIGON

Gerber sat in a metal folding chair at the table set in the center of the room. It was a plywood-paneled room with an air conditioner, which had been paid for by funds taken from a dead VC paymaster and converted on the black market to MPCs. There were fluorescent lights, a fan, filing cabinets and a huge map of Three Corps. In the room with him were Fetterman and Sergeant Derek Kepler, an NCO trained in Intelligence.

"The problem," Gerber began, "is that we don't have much of a clue about this guy. We don't know his name, where he's from or where he's operating. We only know him as Billy the Zip, the name hung on him by Maxwell and the CIA pukes."

Kepler, a burly man with dark hair and a tanned face, was older than most of the soldiers in Vietnam, but not most of the Special Forces soldiers. He was tall, which made him seem lighter than his two hundred pounds. Dressed in faded jungle fatigues and shiny boots, he stored his weapon in the corner within easy reach, in case he decided he needed it for any reason. "I've never heard of anyone called Billy the Zip."

"Yeah," Gerber said, "I don't think the zips would refer to themselves as zips."

"He's into gunfights," said Fetterman. "Sets it up like something out of the wild West. Two men in the street facing each other."

"No," said Kepler, shaking his head slowly. "Doesn't ring a bell."

"It was too good to hope for," said Gerber.

"Just what are you guys doing?" Kepler asked.

Gerber took a deep breath. "Maxwell wants us to locate and eliminate this Billy the Zip. Claims the man is bad for morale, but hell, if no one's heard about him, I don't see how he could be bad for morale."

"He in Three Corps?" Kepler asked.

"Last I heard he was," Gerber answered. "Or rather, that's what Maxwell said."

"I can put out some feelers," Kepler offered. "If he's into this wild West thing for real, then someone out in the field must have heard of him. I'll see what the agents in the villes can come up with."

"What we need is a starting place," Gerber said. "Right now we don't even have that."

"You going after him?" asked Kepler. He glanced at Fetterman and then at Gerber.

"That's the theory," Gerber responded. "Go out and eliminate him before the troops go bug-fuck."

"Am I invited along on this?"

"Hell," said Fetterman, "you can have the whole mission if you want it."

"No, I just want to be in on the end of it."

Gerber stood and pulled his beret out of his pocket. He put it on, careful to center the flash over his eye and then mold the material to the contours of his head. "You ready, Tony?"

"Yes, sir."

"Derek, when...and if you get anything, let me know. We'll be around."

"Yes, sir. I'll get on it as soon as possible."

Gerber and Fetterman left the building. They walked around to the parking lot, and Fetterman climbed into the jeep. He glanced up at the sun and then down at his watch. "Not much time before we're supposed to eat dinner with Robin."

Gerber scratched his chin. "You think we were too subtle with her?"

"No, sir. I think she'll look up anything unusual that's been reported in the past six months. If there's anything there, she'll find it for us."

"Let's get going," said Gerber. He leaned back and put a foot on the dashboard.

Fetterman backed up, twisted around to look over his shoulder, then turned the wheel. Shifting, he pulled forward, stopped, then started again, driving out onto one of the paved streets that crisscrossed the Tan Son Nhut base.

They drove past two-story buildings lined with sandbags. In front of them were small green lawns. Around a few of the lawns were tropical plants, put in after Tet had destroyed the ones that had been there originally. These had been trimmed back so that they provided no cover for attacking VC.

They reached the front gate in time to join the early-evening exodus. Thousands of Vietnamese workers were heading home for the day. Traffic was backed up, but the majority of it was only scooters, motorcycles, Lambrettas and pedestrians. But there were a few trucks and jeeps and two buses.

"Nuts," said Fetterman. "I'd hoped we could avoid all of this."

Gerber glanced at the MP shack where the guards were examining all the parcels being carried out by the Vietnamese. No one wanted the Vietnamese to escape with any government equipment or anything from the PX that could be sold on the black market. It would be a shame if a Vietnamese worker smuggled out an extra carton of cigarettes, a six-pack of beer or a transistor radio.

The line crept forward. Gerber glanced at his watch. "We're going to be late."

"Nothing I can do about it."

"We should have planned this a little better," Gerber said quietly.

One of the buses reached the guards, but it was loaded with GIs and they waved it on through. It belched a black cloud of diesel smoke and rumbled away.

And then Gerber and Fetterman were through the gate and out onto the street. The master sergeant turned to head downtown. They wove their way through the growing evening traffic. The *cao bois* were out in force, the tiny engines of their scooters buzzing like angry bees. Most of them had a girl on the back who wore a short skirt and a form fitting blouse. The *cao bois* ignored the rules of the road, honking and cursing everyone who was in front of them as they dodged along the street.

Fetterman slowed and pulled in behind a taxi that once might have been green or dark blue. It was probably an old Ford, though there were so many Chevy parts on it that it was hard to tell.

Gerber reached up and wiped the sweat from his face, rubbing it on the thigh of his jungle fatigues. He raised a hand to shade his eyes. The street was lined with palms. The trees looked sickly and were probably dying from the pollution in the air or shrapnel damage from Tet or both.

All around them, from the bars and clubs that crowded the street, came the blare of rock and roll or country and western. The music was turned up high to draw the GIs into the clubs, which had names like the Texas Roadhouse, the Colorado River Bar and the New Mexico Bordello. Crowds of GIs, some of them hanging on to Vietnamese girls, waited for an opportunity to enter one of the jam-packed night spots.

"Never changes," Gerber commented.

"And never will," added Fetterman. "Hand a kid a fistful of cash and watch the leeches try to suck it from him. Everyone wants a few of his dollars."

Gerber laughed. "Glad we're too clever to fall for something like that."

"Yes, sir," agreed Fetterman.

Both of them knew it was a lie. They might not be sucked into the clubs where B-girls ordered five-dollar cocktails that might be nothing more than weak tea, but they fell for other gimmicks. Neither had balked at an inflated dinner check. The margin of profit might not have been as great, but both knew they were being taken. And neither of them cared, as long as the food was good.

Fetterman finally pulled over to the curb, reached down and picked up the chain bolted to the floor. He looped it through the steering wheel and used a brass padlock to secure it so that the wheel couldn't be turned. It was the only way to lock the jeep. "The plan now, Captain?"

"We find Robin and eat dinner. We'll see if she's got anything for us."

"Meet you in the lobby in about an hour?"

"Sounds good to me."

WILLIAMS WASN'T SURE that they were going to make it. Chavez was beginning to babble, as if he had lost track of where they were and what was happening to them. He was stumbling along, dragging his feet, and Williams was afraid the enemy would execute him because of his wounds or because he was slowing them down.

Williams whispered into his ear, "Come on, Tomás, you've got to keep up. Stay with me."

And then they stopped. The VC soldiers spread out, surrounding Williams and Chavez, watching them carefully. Williams sat down slowly, helping Chavez. Once they were on the ground, Williams leaned forward toward one of the VC. "We need water."

The man looked at him, but said nothing. Williams repeated the request, this time his voice a little louder. He knew someone would answer him because they would want him to keep quiet.

The leader of the enemy, the man with the western holster appeared. "If you insist on making noise, you'll be eliminated."

"We need water."

"Our glorious soldiers, who destroyed your unit, have no need for water."

"My friend is wounded," said Williams.

"I can end his misery simply."

"A little water," Williams insisted. "What can that hurt?"

"He'll have to wait until we reach camp. If he can't keep up, I'll shoot him."

"Okay, okay," said Williams. He touched the back of his hand to his lips, then wiped the sweat from his face on the sleeve of his fatigues.

"Don't slow us down," the unit commander warned.

With that, the man waved his soldiers to their feet. The point man hurried forward and disappeared into the thick jungle vegetation. They all began to move. Chavez shuffled forward, leaning on Williams. He was soaked with sweat, and there was blood on the side of his uniform, but the bleeding had stopped.

Williams looked at the enemy soldiers directly behind him. A short man in black pajamas carried an old semiautomatic SKS. He looked to be older than most of the enemy soldiers, maybe forty or fifty years old. He returned Williams's gaze but said nothing. He kept walking along, stepping over a fallen log, gliding through the jungle.

Then, suddenly, they stopped again. The man knelt close to Williams, his SKS pointed more or less at him. He grinned, revealing black teeth.

"Jesus," muttered Williams. He glanced at Chavez, who was sitting on the ground, his head hanging down. His breathing was labored and sweat dripped down his face. His skin looked hot and had taken on a waxy, unreal quality. "Chavez? Tomás?"

Chavez opened his eyes briefly. "What?"

"You okay?"

"Water. Need water."

"Soon. Very soon. Just hang on."

Again they got to their feet, but this time they moved only two or three hundred meters. They came out of the heavy undergrowth into an almost parklike area carved out of the triple-canopy jungle. The branches of the trees were woven together overhead, forming a dome of living green. Sunlight didn't filter through at all. Smoke from a cook fire was dissipated by a layered chimney so that four or five feet off the ground it was dispensed.

The patrol moved into the area and fanned out. Williams saw cages suspended above the ground. These were also hootches on poles, some with notched logs leading up into them. And in the center of the camp was a bare, circular area with bleachers on one side. A short stone wall surrounded it.

"You come," one of the captors ordered. "You come or I shoot you."

"Water," said Williams. "We need some water."

The man pushed them toward one of the cages. He held them there until the leader of the enemy came forward. He grinned and said, "You're in for a real challenge."

"My friend needs water," Williams repeated.

The man snapped his fingers, and a soldier appeared, holding a canteen. The officer said, "I'm Captain Nguyen Vo Van and I command here. You are?"

Williams hesitated, then remembered his Code of Conduct training. Name, rank, serial number and date of birth. That was what he was required to give and that was all he had been asked. He gave it quickly.

Van looked down at the wounded man. "You are?"

"Chavez, Tomás. Specialist Four. October 17, 1949."

"Your unit."

Williams shook his head. "Name and rank. You don't get any more."

"Your friend needs water," said Van.

"The Geneva Convention is very specific on that," said Williams.

"Yes, I know it is. And your training is very good, too. But did they tell you that my country didn't sign your agreement? We're not bound by those rules."

For a moment Williams was quiet. Finally he said, "But mine did and I'm bound by them."

"No matter," Van said. "I'm a fair man. I'm an honest man, and I respect your desire not to betray your comrades." He pointed at the soldier with the canteen. "Give Comrade Chavez a small drink."

"Yes, Comrade."

"He should see a doctor."

Van grinned and waved a hand, indicating his small, shabby camp. "We have no doctor. We have no medic. A wounded man is on his own. He either survives his wounds or he dies. It's as simple as that."

"Some medicine for infection," Williams said.

"We have no medicines."

"Yes," Williams argued. "You picked some up from our medic. A bagful."

"Needed for my own soldiers."

Chavez put a hand out, touching Williams on the sleeve of his fatigues. "Don't," he said. "Don't beg."

Van smiled. "No. Don't beg." He then pointed at the hanging cages and fired off an order in Vietnamese, then switched back to English. "I have advised my men to escort you to your new accommodations. Not as luxurious as you've been used to, but they're all we have."

Williams looked up at the cage and shrugged. At the moment there was nothing he could do about it.

MORROW, DRESSED in a pale yellow silk dress, sat up straight, as if she were being interviewed for a job and wanted to make a favorable impression. She ignored the salad sitting on the table in front of her, the wine in the glass that Fetterman had poured moments earlier and the other diners around them. She ignored the decor, the red tablecloths, the white napkins, the red wallpapered walls and the four large windows that overlooked the neon-lit streets of downtown Saigon. She was aware only of Gerber, who stared at her.

"That's all I've heard," she said. "I asked around and there was a story about some Vietnamese, North Vietnamese, who fancied himself a gunfighter."

"Come on," said Gerber, trying to sound as if he didn't believe the story.

She picked up her wineglass, sipped from it, then lowered her voice. "The story is that guys are coming from Cambodia and Thailand to fight him wild West style. He's the man with the rep and everyone wants to knock him off. Just like in all those old cowboy movies. He's supposedly had twenty or thirty of the fights and never even been wounded."

"Who told you this?" Gerber asked.

Morrow raised her eyebrows and grinned. "Can't reveal my sources."

"Where's this guy located?" Fetterman enquired.

"You don't believe the story, do you, Tony?" asked Gerber, continuing the charade.

Fetterman shook his head. "Not really. It's too fantastic. The Old West lives in Vietnam? Pretty funny."

Gerber smiled. "I can't help remembering that this war matches, more closely than anything else, the Indian Wars. Our cavalry posts attacked by hostile Indians. Chases through the wide-open countryside. Maybe it makes a kind of perverse sense."

Morrow laughed. "You guys are after something here." She looked at one and then the other and finally shrugged. "I don't know where he is. Rumors say he's out near the border somewhere. A place where the Cambodians and the Thais can get to him easily, if they want to try their hands at gunning him down, or where he can find refuge if he decides he needs it.''

It was time to change the subject. Gerber ate a bit of his salad and asked, ''Do you have plans for this evening?''

''Nothing that can't be changed,'' she said.

''Well, good,'' said Gerber. ''I don't have any plans, either. Maybe we should make some.''

She picked up her wine, took a sip, then asked, ''Why so coy?''

''Trying to spice things up.''

''Or change the subject.''

''Hey,'' Gerber objected, ''I'm tired of listening to stories of some Vietnamese who thinks he's Billy the Kid.''

''Okay,'' said Morrow. ''Okay, for now.''

Gerber nodded, but didn't like the ominous note in her voice.

HE HAD CLOSED the door of his hotel room and he'd had time to turn and face the interior. The double bed was pushed against one wall, a wardrobe against another wall. The grime-covered window housed an air conditioner. Morrow walked over to it, turned it on, then whirled, facing Gerber. She looked as if she was angry with him. ''Now, just what in hell's going on?''

Gerber shrugged and leaned against the door. He didn't answer the question.

''Mack, we're alone now. We don't have to play games for security.''

Gerber moved deeper into the room and sat down on the only chair. It was a light green and had been repaired with black thread. He leaned forward and unlaced his boots while looking up at Morrow. Kicking them off, he said, "Right now there isn't a lot more to tell. We're interested in learning more about this enemy soldier, and that's really about it. We're just trying to find out if he exists."

"He does," said Morrow. "There wouldn't have been anything from Da Nang if there hadn't been something to those reports. The sources are good ones."

Gerber shrugged. "But right now I'm not very interested in learning anything at all about him. He's a topic that can wait until morning."

"Have you got any Beam's?" she asked.

Gerber stood, walked to the wardrobe and unlocked it. Pushing aside the clean uniforms and the few civilian clothes, he found the bottle and held it up in the light. There was only an inch of liquor in the bottom. "Looks like I'm about out."

"That doesn't matter." She sat down on the edge of the bed, where the feeble breeze from the air conditioner could blow on her. Gerber took a drink from the bottle and handed it to her. She tipped it to her lips, drank, then handed it back. "Thanks. Sometimes you just have to have a drink." She closed her eyes momentarily, then asked again, "Just what in hell's going on?"

"There's not much I can tell you."

"Can't or won't?"

"Can't, right now. We're looking into some things, and if it pans out, I'll get together with you later. We've got to maintain some secrecy. For the moment."

She crossed her legs slowly and nodded. "I'll let you get away with that for now." She tugged at the hem of her dress, pulling it higher, and then uncrossed her legs, giving Gerber a glimpse of thigh. "What I really want to know is whether you've got something else planned for the night."

Glancing at his watch, Gerber shook his head. "I'm clear until morning."

Nodding, Morrow stood up and began to unbutton her dress. She shrugged her shoulders and let the garment slide down her body, pooling around her feet. She stood in front of him, wearing only her bra and panties. The breeze from the air conditioner had dried the sweat. She looked almost comfortable. She ran a hand up her arm, as if feeling the flesh there. Grinning, and then reaching around for the hooks on her bra, she said, "In that case I have a couple of ideas."

Setting the whiskey bottle on the floor, Gerber moved to her. "Let's hear them."

"Okay."

4

HOTEL THREE TAN SON NHUT

Gerber stood in the doorway of the terminal building and watched the helicopters landing and taking off. Hotel Three was a large grassy field with four concrete helipads. It was surrounded by chain-link fence, separating it from the main runways of Tan Son Nhut and from the World's Largest PX, both operated by the Air Force. A group of soldiers, all in jungle fatigues, stood around the entrance of the PX, waiting for it to open. They ignored everything and everyone around them.

"Chopper's inbound now, Captain," said Kepler.

Gerber turned and looked at the intel NCO. "Thanks." He glanced beyond the man and saw the waist-high counter with the bored specialist manning it. Behind him were white scheduling boards recording the tail numbers and destinations of helicopters. Hotel Three served as a bus station. Men returning from leaves, three-day passes or briefings in Saigon converged on Hotel Three and waited for choppers to take them back to their camps. Nothing was officially scheduled, so it was haphazard business. The exceptions were members of the Army Aviation units. They could call their own flight operations and alert them that a ride was needed.

In the waiting area were half a dozen sleeping soldiers. They were sprawled on the two dirty broken-down couches, in a couple of chairs or on the floor. Another half dozen were reading *Playboy* magazines or paperback novels.

Gerber picked up his rucksack and shouldered it. He shifted his weapon to his left hand and stepped out of the terminal and into the hot, humid early morning. Sweat had already soaked his uniform under the arms and down the back, turning it black. He wiped it away and said to Kepler, "It's going to be miserable in the field."

Fetterman joined them, along with two other men— Sergeants Robert Marsh and Charles Laptham. Marsh was a slight man with a perpetual sunburn and peeling skin. He had light brown hair and sharp, distinct features. Laptham was older by two years, had darker hair and a single eyebrow that crossed his face and thinned over the bridge of his pointed nose. The eyebrow seemed to have a life of its own, jumping about as he talked. Laptham had a PRC-25 strapped to his back.

A helicopter appeared just over the top of the PX and descended slowly. The specialist behind the counter yelled, "Hey, Kepler. That's yours."

Kepler waved a hand at the man and shouted back, "Yeah, thanks."

The chopper came to a hover on the farthest of the helipads. The rotor wash tore at the short grass, flattening it. The aircraft swung under its rotor, rocking back and forth until it seemed to fall to the concrete. As it did, the noise of the engine abated and the cyclonic winds disappeared. The crew chief, dressed in faded jungle fatigues and gloves and wearing a flight helmet, jumped to the grass and moved toward Gerber and the others.

As he approached, the man, looking like a giant bipedal insect, yelled, "You Gerber?"

"Captain Gerber. Yes."

"Come on, then. Your ride's here."

Gerber followed the man to the chopper. He climbed up into the cargo compartment, then knelt between the two seats used by the pilots. Pulling a map from his pocket, he pointed at the tiny village of Dong Xoai. "Can you put us down here?"

"We can put you down anywhere, but you sure you want to do that?"

"Not sure I want to do anything, but I have to."

"All right," said the pilot. "That's about a thirty-minute flight."

"Appreciate the lift," said Gerber.

He retreated and sat down on the red canvas troop seat. Fetterman joined him, as did Kepler. Both Laptham and Marsh sat on the floor, looking out the doors.

They lifted to a hover, began a slow climb out over the fence, then turned toward Saigon. When they reached five hundred feet, they turned again and headed off. Gerber got a good look at the turmoil of Saigon. Traffic, both vehicles and people, swarmed the streets. Thousands, hundreds of thousands, strove to get to their jobs or to find a place to spend the day, begging for change. Noise from the traffic, from the people, swelled out, as did the stench of the city. A golden gloom hung over everything, obscuring some of the detail.

Eventually they turned west, following Highway One as the pilot tried to avoid the traffic patterns of Tan Son Nhut. The contrast to the city was amazing. The verdant growth of the jungles extended to the highway on the north. South of the highway was an expanse of swamp. Sunlight reflected from the water, and there was marsh grass as far as the eye could see, an almost unbroken, flat plane with only an occasional clump of trees. In the far distance was a column of blue-white smoke.

They flew around the southern side of the huge American camp at Chu Chi to avoid the gun target lines. The U.S. base squatted among the trees and rice paddies. It was an oval-shaped area that housed thousands of American soldiers, a hospital, an airfield and everything else a small city needed, including a morgue for those who didn't survive their tour.

Beyond it they turned north and crossed the Hobo Woods, heading toward Dau Tieng and the meandering Song Sai Gon. The Hobo Woods wasn't a jungle; it was a forest of stunted trees and thick undergrowth, a tangle of wiry grass and thorny bushes. The red earth showed through, the ground easy to see now. There were American fire support bases, circular camps that housed a battery of 105s or 155s and a couple of infantry companies for protection. These were the outposts that Gerber had been talking about the night before. The American cavalry, a hundred years ago, had hidden behind the walls of their forts. Now, their 1960s counterparts sat on the bunker line, catching the early-morning sun. A few of the GIs looked up and waved as Gerber's chopper flashed overhead.

They detoured to the east of Dau Tieng. In the distance was a rubber plantation, its trees planted in straight rows so that they looked like formations of tall green soldiers marching into battle.

The chopper crossed a couple of roads, which were marked on the map as highways, but which were really little more than dirt tracks. The jungle had been cut back from the shoulders of the roads so that an enemy ambush couldn't be easily established. Mountains, covered with thick jungle, rose up in front of the chopper. To the left was the Song Be.

Kepler tapped Gerber on the shoulder and pointed. "Out there. Dong Xoai."

"That's a pretty big ville."

"Yes, sir. Maybe two, three thousand people. There's a small ARVN garrison charged with keeping the VC out. Fifty or sixty American advisers."

"How are they doing?"

"We've had no reports of any VC activity in the immediate area since the Tet offensive. But from the jungles around it come the rumors of our friend."

"I hope this works," said Gerber, "because I sure as hell don't have a follow-up plan."

The crew chief looked around from his well. "Where do you want to land?"

Gerber glanced at Kepler, who leaned toward the crewman. "Along the road on the north side of the village. Close to the town but outside it."

"You got it."

They circled the town once. It was filled with dung-colored buildings topped by tin and red tile roofs. Many of the streets were narrow and muddy and lined with mud-and-thatch hootches.

They began a descent toward the edge of the road. As they neared it, the rotor wash kicked up red dust, obscuring the town. They hovered for a moment, then settled easily onto the ground.

As the others hopped out, Gerber again crouched between the pilots. "How long can you remain on-station?"

"An hour before we have to go refuel. That takes about thirty minutes or so."

"Before you take off, give us a shout on the radio."

"Yes, sir."

Gerber slid toward the door and climbed out. As he moved off to join the others, the chopper lifted off. It climbed out and took up an orbit at fifteen hundred feet.

Kepler looked at Gerber and the others. "Might be better if I make the rounds by myself."

"I'm not convinced that's a good idea," said Gerber.

"Why not, Captain?" he asked. "I've done it a dozen times before. These people might not be overly friendly, but they're not hostile, either."

"I'd feel better if you had one man as a backup," said Gerber.

Kepler pointed at Marsh. "You're with me, then." He turned to Gerber. "Where are you going to be?"

"Hell, I don't know."

Kepler pointed at a long, low building set back from the road. On the porch were a couple of tables. A Vietnamese girl sat on a chair near the door, watching them. "You can get a Coke there, and I'll be back in a few minutes," the intel specialist said.

Gerber nodded. "Where are you going to be?"

Kepler moved closer and lowered his voice. "I'll be in the house of Vuyen Tri Minh. It's near the center of town, set back from the road with a red tile roof and wall around it. There's a big wooden gate in the wall and a flagpole in the center of the compound."

"Man must be well-off," commented Gerber.

"And that's why he's working with us. Knows that if the VC win, he's going to lose everything he has. He knows that the first thing they'll do is shoot him in the head. He wants to make sure we win."

"You've talked to him before?"

"Oh, yes, sir."

Gerber looked at his watch. "I'll give you an hour, and then we're coming to find you."

"Yes, sir," Kepler said, and moved out with Marsh.

Fetterman moved closer and watched for a moment. Then he rubbed a hand over his face and wiped the sweat on the front of his jungle jacket. "Getting hot."

"Well, let's go get a cold drink," Gerber said. He started toward the hootch that Kepler had pointed out.

The girl, who had been sitting quietly, leaped up and disappeared inside quickly. As they approached, she reappeared with an older, gray-haired woman dressed in black pajamas. She bowed slightly as Gerber stepped up onto the wooden porch. Gerber followed suit.

"You want?"

"Cokes. Three of them."

She nodded and vanished through the door, leaving the girl behind to watch them. Gerber pulled out a chair and sat down. He propped his rifle next to the chair, then reached up under his jungle jacket and pushed at the butt of the Browning M-35 pistol that he wore there. He rarely went into the field without the concealed pistol.

Fetterman and Laptham sat down, too, and as they did, the woman came back, carrying three clear Coke bottles. She opened them in front of the Americans, then stepped back out of the way.

Laptham grabbed a bottle and took a drink, then looked as if he wanted to spit it out. "God, it's almost hot."

Fetterman grinned. "It's a hot country."

"Now, what in hell does that mean?"

Gerber took over. "Not everybody has a fridge."

"It's almost undrinkable," Laptham muttered.

"It's wet," said Fetterman, "and sometimes that's the only thing that matters."

A truck pulled off the road and stopped. Five ARVN soldiers jumped out of the back and three more climbed from the cab. All were dressed in fatigues and each carried an M-16 rifle. They hesitated at the truck, then walked toward the porch. Two of the men stopped at the foot of the steps, holding their weapons loosely. Two more climbed the steps and entered the building. The last four stopped so that they were facing Gerber, Fetterman and Marsh.

"What are you doing here?" asked the ARVN officer, staring at the Americans.

"Having a Coke," Gerber replied.

"Smartass," said the ARVN officer. "I do not need to hear from smartass."

Gerber shrugged. "But that's what I'm doing here. Having a Coke. In a little while we'll be gone, after we finish our Cokes."

"You go now, I think."

Fetterman stared up at the man. "Christ, Captain, this whole country's turning into the wild West."

Gerber took a deep breath and set his Coke bottle down on the table. He turned so that he could grab his M-16 and have a clear shot at the four men facing him if he needed to open fire on them. To the officer, he said, "We're supposed to be allies here. There's no need for any kind of trouble."

"You go now and there be no trouble," said the ARVN, hooking a thumb over his shoulder.

There was a sudden shout from inside the building, followed by a piercing scream. Then more shouting and a slap that sounded like a pistol shot.

Gerber started to rise, but the officer pushed him back roughly. "This is not your business. You stay right here, and no one get hurt."

"They're accusing the woman of being a VC," said Fetterman quietly. "Telling her to admit it or they'll beat her to death."

There was another scream. Gerber glanced at the building and then at the ARVN officer. "Maybe you and your men had better take it easy."

"I do not need advice on how to do my job from you. Finish your drink and get out of here." The officer kept his eyes on Gerber.

The door banged open and the woman stumbled out, falling to the porch. One of the ARVN followed, shouted at her and then turned to the officer, speaking to him rapidly. He then spun and kicked at the woman, who screamed.

"That's enough," snapped Gerber.

The officer whirled on Gerber. "You get out now. Leave your weapons."

"Can't do that," said Gerber.

"You leave weapons and go."

"Nope."

Fetterman stood up and slipped to the right. Two of the ARVN faced him. Laptham moved to the left and watched the men on the ground in front of the porch.

The officer pulled the pistol. "You leave weapons and get out."

The last thing Gerber wanted was to get into a firefight with the ARVN. That would be impossible to explain. Generals, the ambassador in Saigon, everyone, would call and demand answers. None of them would accept the fact that Gerber and the men with him had been pushed into the fight. They'd hang him out in the late-afternoon breeze.

The woman started to moan. She turned a bloody face to Gerber.

"The woman is VC," screamed the ARVN officer.

"Shit," Gerber cursed.

"You go now. Leave weapons." He thumbed back the hammer on his pistol and pointed it at Gerber's midsection. "You get out now."

"Captain," said Fetterman.

Gerber knew he had to act. Staring into the ARVN officer's eyes, Gerber took a step forward, and when the man didn't retreat, Gerber kicked him. His foot snapped up, catching the ARVN in the hand. The pistol flew from his grip. As it did, Gerber stepped in closer and swung his elbow, hitting the officer on the side of the head, just behind the ear. The man groaned once and fell onto his side.

For an instant Gerber thought that was going to be the end of the fight. He thought they had gotten away with it. Then a shot snapped by his head. He dived toward the side of the building, bowling over another of the soldiers there.

A burst of automatic weapons fire erupted. The rounds slammed into the side of the building. Gerber rolled to his right and yanked his pistol from its hiding place. He aimed at one of the ARVN, who seemed to be frozen to the spot, his eyes wide in terror.

Fetterman had leaped to the left and had his rifle up. An ARVN soldier swung his M-16 toward the master sergeant, and Fetterman squeezed off a single shot. There was a piercing scream and the man dropped to the floor, his blood splattering the rough wood.

Laptham leaped over the railing and swung his weapon at the ARVN soldiers there. One of them started to retaliate, but then froze. Both dropped their rifles and raised their hands above their heads.

Gerber scrambled to his feet. The ARVN officer was standing now, his face a mask of hatred, but he didn't move or speak.

"Tony?"

"Fine, sir."

"Laptham?"

"Okay, Captain."

Gerber looked at the soldier still on the ground. He was lying on his side, blood pumping from his wound. His face was waxy-looking, his eyes unfocused. He was dying rapidly and there wasn't anything they could do for him.

To the ARVN officer, Gerber said, "Now, get your men and get out of here. And leave your weapons, or we're going to take them away from you."

The ARVN officer remained motionless, his hands out, palms down, looking as if he were measuring all the angles. He glanced at Fetterman and then at Marsh.

"Get out," commanded Gerber.

The ARVN snapped an order to his men. Two of them grabbed the body of the dead man, lifting him under the arms and by the ankles. They carried him down the steps and toward the parked truck.

For a moment the others stood there, staring at the Americans. Then, one by one, they turned, walking toward the street. Finally the ARVN officer whirled and stormed off the porch.

Fetterman moved closer to Gerber. "What are we going to do now?"

Gerber laughed. "I think we'd better get Kepler and get the hell out of here before that officer comes back with a whole company."

"Sounds like a good plan to me," said Fetterman.

5

THE JUNGLES NEAR
THUAN LOI

It had been an uncomfortable night. The huge cage swung with each movement, making Williams slightly seasick. It wasn't big enough to stand in or long enough to lie in, and the floor, which was made of bamboo poles four inches apart, wouldn't allow him to sit in one position for more than a few minutes. He had to move constantly, and that made the cage swing, which in turn made him sick to his stomach.

Chavez hadn't been subjected to the indignity of the hanging cages, because his wound made it difficult for him to remain conscious. There was no point in torturing a man if he couldn't appreciate the pain of the torture. Instead, he had been locked in a hootch. Only occasionally was he conscious enough to groan, and once he had screamed.

Williams had spent the night shifting and moving and turning and twisting, wishing it was morning so that they would let him out, if only for a few minutes. Just long enough to stretch.

The VC soldiers had spent the night as soldiers everywhere did. They'd listened to the radio, the voice of the announcer quiet and the music almost impossible to hear. Guards had been sent out at dusk while others had come in. Men sat in small groups and ate meals of rice and fish heads. They talked and joked, their weapons within easy grasp. They paid no attention to Williams or anything else around them now that they were off duty.

As the last of the light had faded, a soldier had come from the headquarters and walked up to the swinging cage. Williams had turned to look and noticed that this soldier was a woman. Her black hair fell to her waist. She wore Ho Chi Minh sandals on her dirty feet, black shorts, and a black silk shirt that was tight enough to prove she was a woman.

For a moment she'd stood there, examining Williams, and then turned and walked away. She hadn't spoken, smiled or even indicated she'd recognized him as human. Williams had noticed a white scar on the back of her thigh as she'd left.

The remainder of the night was spent swinging around. The activity in the camp had dropped off. As morning came, the noise in the jungle increased. Birds took to flight, monkeys shrieked and the other animals howled. Insects swarmed, making life even more miserable for him. As the mosquitoes attacked, he found he didn't have the strength to fight them off.

At dawn the soldiers who had been in the field returned. Others left their quarters, some of them walking by the cage to look up at Williams, shouting comments at him, taunting him. Suddenly he felt like an animal in a zoo. All he wanted was out, to escape, but he didn't want them to see that he wanted out. He sat as quietly as possible, the pain from the bamboo poles burning into his legs and back, but he didn't want them to know that.

One of the VC pointed, laughed and pulled a piece of bread from his pocket. He held it out, as if offering food to an animal in a cage. He waved it, trying to get Williams's attention, and finally, in frustration, threw it at him, hitting him in the chest.

Williams ignored that, too. He wanted to get out of the cage so that he could relieve himself. He was thirsty, tired and hungry, too, but he didn't want his captors to know any of that. He wanted out, but not enough to beg them.

At midmorning, when Williams thought he couldn't stand the agony any longer, he knew he'd have to piss in front of everyone and ask them for some water. At that moment Van emerged from the headquarters building. He stopped at the foot of the cage, looked up and studied Williams. "You don't look so good, my American friend."

"I'm tired."

"Yes. I'm afraid the accommodations are less than adequate, but I'm sure you understand."

"Let me out."

Van nodded, then grinned. He turned to one of the guards and spoke in Vietnamese. The guard moved forward and worked at the chain and the lock on the door. He swung it wide, then stepped back, his weapon up and ready.

"You may exit," said Van.

Williams tried to move, but pain shot through his body. He reached under himself and lifted, sliding forward carefully until his feet were extended beyond the door. Then he grabbed the side of the door and pulled himself forward until he was sitting on the edge.

Slowly Williams eased himself out of the cage, reaching down with his toes until his feet touched earth. When he was on the ground, he carefully straightened up, his back stiff from the position he'd been forced to assume the night before. He tried not to groan in pain, tried not to show any emotion.

"You may have something to eat, relieve yourself and clean up," Van told him.

"Thank you."

"Your friend," said Van, "has had a rough night. He needs medical assistance."

"I know," said Williams. "What can I do to help him?"

"Your unit and your mission."

"The Geneva Convention dictates that I give you no information of military value."

Van shrugged. "I've told you that we didn't sign the Geneva Convention. And while we argue over political points, your friend suffers. Why not help him and worry about the politicians later?"

"I have a Code of Conduct to follow," said Williams. "I can't violate that."

"Then your friend will continue to suffer." Van stopped, as if deep in thought. "Maybe there is a way, however. If you're brave enough."

"What?"

"No," said Van. "It's not right. Forget it."

"Please, I'll do anything I can to help him as long as I don't have to betray my unit or my friends."

"Why don't you have breakfast first?" suggested Van. "Then we can discuss this."

"But my friend needs help now."

"We'll do what we can. Come along with me."

Williams took a step forward, afraid his ankles and knees wouldn't be able to support his weight. There was a tingling in his legs as the blood began to flow again. He stood for a moment, gritted his teeth, then took a second step.

"Come, we'll find you something to eat and then we'll talk about the price of assistance."

As soon as the ARVN had driven off, Gerber pointed at Laptham. "Get on the horn and get the chopper in here. Have it land in front of us."

"Yes, sir."

"What about Kepler and Marsh?" asked Fetterman.

"We'll get in the chopper and then see if we can't find them from the air."

"We're going to have to get the women out of here, too," said Fetterman. "The ARVN will come back and kill them."

Gerber looked at the woman sitting on the porch. She was staring at them. The girl who had served them stood in the doorway, looking as if she had been frozen in place.

Laptham interrupted. "Chopper's inbound."

"Gather the weapons and take them with you," Gerber told Laptham. He moved to the woman and helped her to her feet. "You're going to have to come with us."

"I stay."

"You stay and they'll kill you. They think you're selling information to the VC."

"I stay."

Gerber nodded, but then pointed at the young girl. "They'll rape and kill your daughter. You want that to happen?"

"I stay. We find help."

The sound of rotors interrupted them. Gerber looked up and then back at the woman. "We can take you anywhere you want to go."

"My home here. I stay."

"Knowing that the ARVN will be back?"

"They look for you. They no longer care about me. I stay here."

The helicopter was closer, noisier. Laptham had moved nearer to the road. He turned suddenly and yelled, "We got a problem, Captain. Two trucks coming at us, moving fast. I think our ARVN friend is about to return. And this time he's got plenty of help."

"Shit." Gerber moved off the porch, closer to the road. He grabbed the last of the weapons left by the ARVN and slung it. Pointing at Laptham, he said, "Tell the pilots to hurry and that the LZ might be hot."

"They're going to love that." Laptham spoke into the handset. "Ah, let's hurry it up. We've got some unfriendly ARVNs coming at us."

The chopper seemed to fall out of the sky then, diving for the ground. It leveled out near the road, hovering along it at high speed. A cloud of red dust followed the chopper, obscuring the trucks that were coming toward them.

Gerber faced the woman. "This is your last chance. You'd better come along."

"I stay. This my home."

Gerber nodded, understanding her desire to stay. It had kept the Jews in Nazi Germany long after many knew they should have gotten out. It kept people in the paths of hurricanes when those with good sense had left. People stayed with their homes and with their neighbors, reluctant to leave what was familiar.

The helicopter flared in front of them, then dropped to the ground. As it did, Laptham ran forward and leaped up into the cargo compartment.

"Captain!" yelled Fetterman. He held two extra M-16s by their iron sights.

Gerber saw that the trucks were now no more than two hundred yards away, creating a cloud of dust themselves. Men were standing behind the cabs, pointing at the chopper. One man had raised his weapon.

Gerber glanced at the woman and knew that the only thing he could do was drag her to the chopper. She didn't want to go and wasn't afraid of the ARVN.

There was a burst of automatic weapons fire. One of the ARVN had an M-16 pointed over the top of the cab. Gerber didn't know where the rounds were going. They didn't hit the chopper and didn't come close to him. The trucks hadn't stopped. They were bearing down on the helicopter, the men in the rear now screaming at the tops of their voices.

Gerber sprinted toward the road and crossed it. As he leaped for the cargo compartment, Fetterman leaned out to help him up. The helicopter lifted off as his feet touched the skids. Then the nose dropped and they began to race along the road.

"Taking fire!" yelled the crew chief. He stepped out and turned, his M-60 aimed rearward at the approaching ARVN.

"Don't shoot!" yelled Gerber. "Don't shoot."

The nose came up and all of them were thrown back. Gerber fell and grabbed at the leg of the troop seat to keep from sliding to the side. Behind them, he could hear the hammering of M-16s as the ARVN fired at the helicopter, trying to bring it down.

And then they were out of range. The crew chief fell back into his well. He glanced out at Gerber. The chopper leveled and one of the pilots looked back.

Gerber moved to the front and said, "I've got two men down there still."

"Where?"

"Near the center of town. We've got to get them out before the ARVN find them."

"We're going to have to hurry," said the pilot. "We're running low on fuel."

"I know where they are. Just turn it around and we'll get them out."

"Here we go," he said.

ALTHOUGH THEY DIDN'T LET him have complete privacy, he didn't have the whole camp watching as he relieved himself. He finished that and felt better. It was funny how the little things could make everything else seem trivial. With his bladder empty and the promise of breakfast, he was feeling much better than he had during the long night. Better than any time since he'd been captured. He walked around to where Van waited for him. "Now what?" he asked the enemy commander.

"Come."

Van led him to one of the hootches at the edge of the camp. He was taken inside, where there were two long, rough-hewn tables. Metal bowls sat on the table, and at the far end of the hootch was an open-hearth fireplace.

"Sit," said Van.

Williams climbed over the bench and sat down. A Vietnamese in black pajamas set a bowl of rice in front of him. It was steaming hot, and there was a thick gruel at the bottom of it. The breakfast wasn't the best he'd eaten, but it was hot food, and Williams knew he'd want to keep his strength up if he was going to escape. That was the first time he'd thought about escape. Until then he'd only been thinking about keeping Chavez from being executed.

Van sat next to him and watched him eat. He snapped his fingers once, and the man returned with a canteen of water, which he set in front of Williams. "Drink," said Van.

Williams dropped his wooden spoon and picked up the canteen. The water was tepid, but he didn't care. He drank gratefully, stopping to breathe, and then drank again. Leaning forward, his face no more than four inches from the bowl of rice, he shoveled it in as fast as he could eat, suddenly afraid they'd take it away.

"Slow down," said Van.

Williams looked at him, then sat back. He chewed the rice and swallowed. "I didn't realize how hungry I was."

"If you eat too fast, you'll throw it back up. Eat slowly."

"Yes, sir," said Williams, not realizing what he was saying. When he finished the rice and water, he pushed the bowl away, then looked at Van. "I appreciate the hot food."

"That was the total ration for one man for an entire day," said Van. "You Americans have so much. You waste so much and never realize how good you have it. We have so very little in comparison."

"We earned it," said Williams. "Through hard work and sacrifice and innovation. We earned everything we have."

"Your Indians might disagree with that," said Van.

"The strong always impose their will on the weak."

"That doesn't make it right," said Van.

Williams nodded. "But it's no different than your soldiers forcing a village to pay taxes and to support your cause. The strong ruling the weak."

"That's what you think?" asked Van. "That we have to force people to support us?"

"I've seen it."

"No, my young friend, you've seen nothing but the propaganda written by the puppet soldiers in Saigon. You've seen nothing but the lies your government has told to deceive you."

Williams remained silent. He didn't know what to say. There was the possibility that the government could lie to him about what was happening. He'd seen none of the atrocities himself. He'd heard stories and seen some pictures and had accepted, as true, the stories of VC tax collectors because there was no reason to question what he had been told.

"Would you like to leave here?" asked Van. "Take your wounded friend and get out?"

"Of course," he said.

"Then I have a proposition for you. Agree, and you might be able to leave tomorrow. Refuse, and I'm afraid I'll be forced to hang you."

"You can't do that," said Williams. He spoke calmly, as if he didn't believe a word of what he was hearing. He'd been told in his Code of Conduct classes that the enemy would lie to him. Refuse to cooperate and it might be difficult at first, but finally they would give up. Once they learned he wouldn't cooperate they'd leave him alone.

"I can do anything I want," said Van. "I'm here in the jungle and no one will ever know what happened. All your comrades are dead now. You're missing in action. I can make that a permanent state. Your family and friends won't know what happened to you. Perhaps they'll think you vanished in the jungles of Vietnam, fleeing the fight in cowardice.''

''I can't help you,'' Williams said quietly.

''I know that. But I'm giving you the opportunity to save your own life and that of your wounded comrade.''

''What do I have to do?''

''Ah,'' said Van, ''an intelligent young man. You don't refuse until you've heard the proposition. It's simple, really. It's a chance to escape with your life.''

Williams sat there speechless, staring at the empty rice bowl and feeling nauseated.

''It's a game I play. A simple game, patterned after the games of your Old West. You win, you walk away. You lose, you stay here.''

''Go on.''

''Two men face each other. Each has a pistol. On the count of three, each draws and fires. Only one man survives. Only one man walks away.''

''A gunfight? You want me to face you in a gunfight?''

''It's as simple as that.''

Williams was silent for a moment, then asked, ''What choice do I have?''

''I told you. You can face me and win your freedom, or you can hang after you watch me shoot your wounded friend through the head.''

Williams was silent for a moment. Sweat beaded on his face, and he swiped at it with the palm of his hand. The gunfight was against the rules of land warfare, against the rules of civilization, but none of that seemed to matter here. The rules were written by the man with the highest rank. Van controlled this section of the jungle, and Williams had to play by his rules.

The Code of Conduct gave him the answer. According to it, American soldiers didn't play games with the enemy. They didn't get into debates about the relative merits of political systems or into discussions about the legality of the war in Vietnam. Name, rank, serial number and date of birth was it. Absolutely no gunfights.

"You'll hang," said Van. "For war crimes. Remember, we captured you standing over the body of one of our men whom you had just killed."

"That was war."

"Tell it to his friends. Tell it to his family." Van hesitated, then said, "But you have a choice. A fair fight or hanging."

For a moment Williams couldn't accept the situation. No one staged gunfights anymore. Those had died out with the last of the Old West marshals and outlaws. It was a fiction of the movies. It was a half-truth about the way the West had supposedly been.

He turned and looked into Van's face. The Vietnamese seemed eager for his answer. His eyes glowed in anticipation of the coming fight. The man thought he was Wyatt Earp, facing down the Clantons at the O.K. Corral.

"I have no choice," said Williams.

"You can hang."

"No," he said finally. "I'll go along with you, but only if you guarantee that I'll go free, with Tomás, if I win."

"You have my word."

"Then I'll do it."

6

DONG XOAI, RVN

They circled the village at two hundred feet. Out the cargo compartment door Gerber could see the mud-choked streets, the thatched hootches and the people wearing black pajamas. There were a few military people, all of them carrying obsolete weapons such as M-1 carbines.

"There!" shouted Fetterman. "I've got them at three o'clock on the road."

Gerber slid over and looked down. Kepler and Marsh were walking along the road, side by side. Gerber leaned forward and yelled at the copilot, "Can we land and pick them up?"

The man glanced out the windshield, then nodded. He touched the pilot on the shoulder and pointed at the two Special Forces troopers.

The helicopter banked suddenly and dived at the road. Gerber fell back and laughed. At least Kepler wouldn't open fire. There was no way the VC would come at him in a Huey. Maybe out of a hootch or the jungle, or even out of a tunnel, but not in a chopper.

Kepler glanced up, then clamped his hand over his green beret. He turned away from the aircraft, bowing his head against the onslaught of wind and swirling dirt that washed over him.

The chopper hovered ten or twelve feet above the ground, then settled slowly onto the road. As it touched down, the rotor wash dissipated. Kepler whirled and ran toward the chopper, leaping into the rear. He spotted Gerber, who was now sitting on the troop seat. "What's going on, Captain?"

"We had to get out."

"Why?"

Before Gerber could answer, Marsh scrambled into the cargo compartment and the chopper lifted off. It climbed out to the east, trying to keep away from the nearby ARVN base.

"We had some trouble with the ARVN," Gerber told Kepler. "Did you learn anything important?"

Kepler shrugged. "Not really. There are rumors of a VC camp around here somewhere, but hell, everywhere you go there are rumors of a VC base. Nothing new."

"Billy the Zip?" asked Gerber.

"Nothing, Captain. Rumors of some wise guy VC, but nothing concrete. Nothing that would help us launch a search around here for him."

They continued to climb out, reaching fifteen hundred feet and leveling off. Kepler crouched near the cargo compartment door and looked down at the deep greens of the jungle and the lighter greens of the rice paddies, almost as if searching for the rumored camp of Billy the Zip. Finally he moved back and sat down on the troop seat. "So, what happened?" he shouted over the roar of the wind and the turbine of the Huey.

Gerber shook his head. Leaning in close, he said, "I'll fill you in when we get back to Saigon."

Kepler held up a thumb and nodded.

Gerber turned his attention to the landscape of Vietnam sliding under them. Now they followed the Song Sai Gon as it meandered toward the capital. There were now hundreds of aircraft flying around—jet fighters, helicopters, spotter planes and transports. The skies over Vietnam were as busy as many of the roads back in the World. In Vietnam an aircraft was as common as a car.

They approached Saigon from the northwest over the spreading floodplain of the Song Sai Gon. It looked a mile wide and no deeper than an inch or two. The ground around it had been torn up by the construction of a dozen different projects, and unlike the rest of Vietnam, this area looked as if it belonged somewhere else.

They turned and followed a four-lane divided highway that led from Bien Hoa to Saigon. Then they broke to the west and made their approach to Hotel Three, swooping over the top of the World's Largest PX and landing on a concrete pad. As Gerber started to move, the crew chief tapped him on the shoulder. "AC wants to talk to you."

Gerber went forward and crouched near the console between the two pilots. The aircraft commander removed his helmet, holding it in both hands as if it were a crown. He wiped the sweat from his forehead on the sleeve of his jungle fatigues. "What are we supposed to report about taking fire?" he asked.

Gerber shrugged. "You take any hits?"

"Nothing showed up on the instruments. I didn't feel anything hit the aircraft, but sometimes when they pass through the tail boom you don't feel it."

"So don't report anything," said Gerber.

"I don't want any of our people landing there, thinking the village is friendly and then getting shot to shit."

"Those were ARVN troops shooting and they weren't shooting at you, but at us. I'm afraid we pissed them off. Follow-up missions should have no trouble."

The pilot shook his head, then ran a gloved hand through his sweat-damp hair. "I really should advise my operations about the incident."

"You do whatever you think's right," said Gerber.

"I will."

"Thanks for the lift. I appreciate you getting us out of that mess."

The pilot laughed. "Anything for a fellow American."

Gerber climbed out of the chopper and started across the grass of Hotel Three. He caught up with Fetterman and Kepler at the door to the terminal. Both Laptham and Marsh were standing off to one side.

"Tony, let's you and me head over to MACV and see what we can learn there. Derek, you go back over to SOG and see if there's anything there that might help."

"I think we've shot our wad, Captain," said Kepler.

"I do, too, but let's play out this final hand before we pack it in."

"Yes, sir."

He turned to the other two men. "Thanks for your help. Are you going to be around for a few days?"

Laptham grinned. "Nothing coming up, and I'm not about to volunteer for anything that would take me out of Saigon. Rather be here than out in the field."

"Then hang loose. I might need you again in a couple of days."

"Sure thing, Captain."

Kepler, Laptham and Marsh moved off, walking out the gate and turning down the road that would take them past the World's Largest PX.

"Now what?" asked Fetterman.

"Let's head over to see Jerry Maxwell."

"Are you going to tell him what happened out there this morning?"

"I think that's for the best. I don't want him learning about it from the ARVN."

"Well, sir, I'm right behind you."

MAXWELL SAT AT HIS DESK, listening quietly as Gerber outlined the morning's mission for him. Maxwell said nothing during the narration, though he did raise his eyebrows once when Gerber talked about shooting it out with the ARVN. He looked from one man to the other, then asked, "You actually killed an ARVN soldier?"

"Knock it off, Jerry," said Fetterman, annoyed. "They started it."

"You sound like a kid talking about a fight on the playground."

"Look, Maxwell," said Gerber, "I'm not going to get into a debate over the ARVN. They drew down on us and wanted our weapons. That's something we don't do. We don't surrender our weapons."

"In the interest of international relations and our relations with the ARVN," said Maxwell, "you could have surrendered them. Hell, we've plenty of them."

"No," said Gerber. "That is one thing we don't do. No one takes our weapons from us. A soldier who surrenders his weapons easily, at the whim of others, isn't a soldier."

"Come on," said Maxwell, smiling, his voice light. "You're making more of this than necessary."

"Jerry," said Fetterman, "you're the one who doesn't understand. No one takes my weapon away from me. Period. Not ever."

Maxwell looked from one man to the other, not understanding. It seemed to be such a trivial thing. Surrender the weapon and no one has to die. Now they had an ARVN soldier dead because Gerber and Fetterman subscribed to some warrior's code that wouldn't allow them to give up their weapons without a fight.

Looking from one man to the other, he said, "It seems to be a point you didn't need to fight over. They weren't going to shoot you on the spot."

"Can you guarantee that, Jerry?" asked Gerber. "How do you know that the moment we surrendered our weapons they wouldn't have opened fire? No, on this point we stand firm. We don't surrender our weapons to anyone."

Maxwell sat back and shook his head. "If Fetterman asked for your weapon, you wouldn't give it to him?"

"Different situation," said Gerber. "I trust Sergeant Fetterman. He wants my weapon, he can have it. I don't trust the ARVN, and the only way they'll ever get my weapon is if they kill me first."

"Stupid," said Maxwell. "Just plain stupid."

"How is it stupid?" asked Gerber. "A bunch of people show up wearing ARVN uniforms, but they could just as easily be VC. I don't know who they are, but if they're my allies, they know I'm authorized to have the weapon. There's no reason to give it to them. They draw on us, thinking that by waving their rifles at us, we'll give up. That didn't work, either. So tough shit on them."

Maxwell shrugged, then waved his hand as if trying to erase the line of discussion. "So, while you were there, did you learn anything about our man?"

"Nope," said Gerber. "No one's heard anything concrete. We dug up some rumors about it, and those ARVN idiots this morning acted and sounded as if they'd just come out of the Old West, but other than that, nothing."

"You know, Captain," said Fetterman, "you just said something that makes me wonder if maybe Billy the Zip isn't an ARVN."

"No way," objected Maxwell.

"Why not?" asked Fetterman. "We got a posse coming at us like western marshals, demanding we surrender our guns while in town. We have what amounts to a wild West gunfight right there in the street. Billy the Zip would have loved it if he'd been there."

"The ARVN would never allow one of their men to operate that way."

"Oh, hell," said Gerber. "Half the time the ARVN can't tell you who they've got on their rosters. We've had a lot of hot dogs running around out there."

Turning back to Fetterman, Maxwell said, "From the limited information we have, I don't think Billy's an ARVN."

"Well," said Gerber, "I haven't, we haven't, been able to come up with anything at all. We tried the one lead we had, and it went nowhere. If Billy the Zip is VC or NVA, he could be hiding out in the jungle where we'd never find him, or he might just slip across the Cambodian border where he'd be safe from us. Without more I can't see any point in continuing to search for him."

"We have to do something about him," said Maxwell.

"Hell, Jerry, you can't even prove he exists. We could be chasing a phantom."

"You refusing to help me now?"

"No, Jerry, I'm telling you the facts of life. If there's nothing more you can tell me, then there's nothing more we can do."

"You going to be around Saigon for the next few days?" Maxwell asked.

"We've got no plans to hit the field," Gerber said.

"Then, if I come up with something more, you'll take a look at it?"

Gerber nodded. "If you have something substantial, but I doubt you're going to get it. This thing smacks of a story intended to scare people." He stood up.

"I'll be in touch," said Maxwell.

"Wait a minute," said Fetterman. "What about this shoot-out with the ARVN?"

"They know who you are?"

"I doubt that," said Gerber. "We were just three GIs having a Coke."

"Then don't worry about it. If I hear anything, I'll let you know."

Gerber started toward the door, then stopped. "One thing you might do is find out what happened to the Vietnamese women. Make sure they haven't carted them off or that they didn't shoot them on the spot."

"I'll look into it."

Gerber opened the door and stepped into the corridor. He waited until Fetterman joined him. As they walked along, Fetterman asked, "So we're going back to the hotel now?"

"I figure that's the best plan, unless you've got a couple of ideas."

"No, sir. I'm still bothered by this Billy the Zip thing, though. Seems like there should be something more we could do about it."

"If he really exists," said Gerber. "We can't even prove that right now."

"So, what are we going to do?"

"The only thing we can. Hang loose."

"Yes, sir."

7

THE JUNGLES NEAR
THUAN LOI

Williams, having agreed to the gunfight, wasn't put back in the swinging cage. Instead, he was allowed into the hootch where Chavez lay on a bamboo mat, groaning occasionally and sweating continuously. It didn't look as if anyone had examined the wounded man since they had arrived at the camp the day before. Chavez still wore his bloodstained uniform. His face was dirty and he was soaked with sweat.

Williams crouched near him and reached out but didn't touch him. He looked into his eyes and then at the bullet hole in his shirt. "Oh, man."

Chavez's eyes seemed to focus, and then the lids fluttered. For an instant it seemed as if he was going to recognize Williams, but then his eyes rolled up and he fell back, unconscious, his breath ragged.

"You take it easy," said Williams. "I'll get you some help." He stepped to the door of the hootch and saw Van standing in the distance, talking to another soldier. "Hey!" he shouted. "We need a medic here."

Van looked at him, said something to the soldier, then started to move toward the hootch. As he neared it, he said, "You keep shouting and I'll shoot you now. We must be quiet out here."

"Sorry, but my friend needs some help."

Van entered the hootch, knelt near the wounded American and turned his face away, wrinkling his nose. "Your friend smells very bad."

"My friend needs some help, or he's going to die. If you don't get him some assistance, I'm not going to participate in your gunfight."

"All right." He moved back to the door and waved a hand at his soldiers outside. Turning to Williams, he said, "Help is on the way."

Williams looked out the door. The camp was still wrapped in shadows, the sun failing to penetrate the thick canopy over it. Smoke from the fire hung in the air at about eye-level, giving everything a slightly blue cast.

A shadow fell across the door, and a man carrying a medic's bag, stolen from the Americans, entered. He crouched near Chavez, studied him, then touched his forehead. Leaning forward, he picked at the blood-stained fabric near the bullet hole, trying to see the wound. Finally he opened the bag and searched through it. As he did, he said to Van in Vietnamese, "I'd like a pan of water and a clean cloth."

Van hesitated, looking from the medic to Chavez and then at Williams. He turned and stepped out, calling quietly in Vietnamese. A moment later a man appeared and handed a pan to Van, who carried it to the medic.

"Set it down there," the medic said in Vietnamese.

Van did as he was told, then stepped back. To Williams he said, "Maybe we should leave."

"I want to help."

The medic ignored the two men. He carefully unbuttoned Chavez's jungle jacket, pulling it away from the blood-encrusted wound. Williams stared down at it, shook his head and groaned slightly. Chavez's shoulder was bruised. It had turned dark purple, and the wound itself was star-shaped and blackened. It looked as if the barrel of the enemy weapon had been pressed against his body when the trigger was pulled.

Using the cloth, the medic gently washed the wound, at first smearing the dried blood. He cleaned it, thoroughly rinsing the cloth in the pan, which turned the water rust-colored. When he finished cleaning the bullet hole, he dug through the bag and pulled out sulpha powder, sprinkling it liberally on Chavez's shoulder. Done with that, he shook out a field dressing and bandaged the wound easily.

"That it?" asked Williams.

"Be patient," said Van. "It's all we can do for him. It's all we could do for one of our own soldiers."

"Don't you have to remove the bullet?" asked Williams.

"Help me," said the medic in response. He had moved into a position so that he was kneeling next to Chavez. His hands were under the man's shoulder and waist. "I want to roll him onto his stomach," he told Williams.

Williams moved around and knelt next to the medic. Together they rolled Chavez over. Chavez didn't make a sound. He rolled onto his belly and lay as still as death.

The medic pulled the jungle jacket free and tossed it aside. Chavez's back looked as if he had been rolling in mud. It was covered with dirt and dried blood. The exit wound was a small, neat hole, which indicated that there was no bullet to remove. There were a few strips of skin blown away from the wound, but it wasn't much larger than a normal entrance wound.

Again the man cleaned the wound, sprinkled sulpha powder and bandaged Chavez. Then he stood and said to Van, "I don't think we should move him again now."

"Can't you give him a shot?" Williams asked Van.

"A shot of what?"

Williams shrugged. "I don't know. What has your medic got in that bag?"

"There's nothing more he can do for your friend."

"Antibiotics," said Williams. "He needs something to fight the infection. There's going to be an infection, and he'll need antibiotics."

"We have no antibiotics," said Van. "We've done all we can. Later, we'll see that he gets the food and water he needs and our doctor, when he returns, will check on him periodically." Van grinned. "Now, there are some things that must be done before we have our contest. Come with me."

Together they stepped out of the hootch and into the dim green glow of the jungle.

MORROW HAD NOTHING to do for lunch. Gerber learned that when he stopped in at her office in Saigon. He'd been by the building once before, but had never been inside it. Usually he met Morrow on the street when she got off work for the day. Fetterman now sat in the jeep parked in the shade at the curb, waiting quietly for Gerber to return.

Gerber walked up to the door, grabbed it and found it locked. On the wall was a small speaker with a black button under it. Gerber pushed the button and waited.

"Yeah," said a tinny voice.

Gerber glanced back at Fetterman. "Captain Gerber to see Robin Morrow."

"You wait."

A moment later Robin's voice came over the speaker. "Mack? That you?"

"Yeah. You want to get some lunch with Tony and me?"

"Can you wait a minute?"

"Sure."

"Then I'll be right down. Don't get impatient and run off. Okay?"

"I'll be waiting." He turned and walked back to the jeep, climbing into the passenger side.

"She coming?" Fetterman asked.

"In a minute."

Gerber sat quietly. When there was a noise from the door, he turned. Morrow, wearing her standard jumpsuit outfit with the sleeves rolled up and the legs hacked off at midthigh, appeared. She was carrying her camera bag, which she set in the rear of the jeep before hopping up and into the back of the vehicle. Leaning forward, she said, "Mack, I've found out a little more about that gunfighter."

Gerber turned in the seat. Fetterman didn't start the engine. He sat there quietly, listening to everything Morrow said.

"Seems he might be down around I Corps," she told them. "There were rumors of someone around there getting into cowboy gunfights."

"VC or NVA?" asked Gerber.

"That's never been established for certain, though the thinking at the time was that he had to be NVA. The VC wouldn't have the education for it."

Gerber glanced at the sidewalk, where pedestrians walked quietly. There was traffic in the street, the normal assortment of jeeps, trucks, cars, Lambrettas and scooters. There were hundreds of people to overhear their conversation, though no one seemed interested in anything they said. If he cautioned her about security, she would know there was something going on and would want more information. The best thing was just to let her talk as the mood moved her. "What do you mean the VC wouldn't have the education?" he asked.

She touched him on the shoulder. "The story I get, and this comes from our bureau out of Da Nang, is that the guy knows all about the American West. I mean, he knows it well. Not the tripe from Hollywood, but the real stories behind some of the real events. That would indicate a good education, and the majority of the Vietcong don't have that kind of higher education."

Gerber knew there were VC from the upper classes of South Vietnam who had been exposed to higher education in France, England and the United States, but he didn't argue about the point. Instead, he asked, "How do they know so much?"

"The man began to brag about what he was doing. He'd shoot his mouth off in the villages and hamlets, and that information got back to American Intelligence sources, who prepared some kind of a report about it all—classified, of course."

Gerber wiped the sweat from his forehead and looked at Morrow. She seemed to be cool enough in her abbreviated costume. "But one of your reporters got his hands on it, anyway?"

"I think it was leaked on purpose. Anyway, the guy was bragging and leaving challenges around, trying to draw some Americans out to fight him. That never worked. He then started leaving bodies outside the American camps with a number pinned to them. I guess that was the number of the man he killed. He shot fifteen of them in I Corps.''

"Is there anything on paper about this?" Fetterman questioned.

"You don't believe me?" asked Morrow.

Fetterman shrugged. "I just wondered how much information about this was available."

"You could check through your own Intelligence channels," suggested Morrow.

Fetterman started the jeep, glanced over his shoulder and pulled out into the traffic. "Where are we going?"

"Mack said something about lunch," said Morrow. "That's what I'm counting on."

Fetterman turned a corner, and they drove down a wide street filled with traffic. There were thousands of people, noise from the traffic and music blaring from a dozen bars and clubs. The air was heavy with the stench of diesel fumes and humidity. Conversation was impossible. Morrow sat back in the rear of the jeep. Gerber rode with one foot on the dashboard, watching the crowds swirling around them.

They turned a second corner, and Fetterman dived out of the traffic, aiming at a parking place that opened up as a taxi pulled away. He stopped and turned off the engine, picking up the chain from the floorboards to loop through the steering wheel. Securing it with a padlock, he asked, "Lunch at the Continental Shelf?"

"Of course," said Morrow.

She grabbed her camera bag and climbed out the back. Gerber retrieved his rifle and joined her on the sidewalk. When Fetterman stepped toward them, they began to walk toward the outdoor restaurant known as the

Continental Shelf. Morrow walked on ahead of them, mixing with the crowds on the sidewalk.

When she was ahead of them, Fetterman touched Gerber on the shoulder. "Now what?"

Gerber knew what Fetterman was talking about. They had come from Maxwell's office, convinced there was nothing to the story of Billy the Zip. Nothing to go on, at least. The whole thing was a dead end that didn't require any more research. Now Morrow had given them proof that something was happening. The man had moved from I Corps down to Three Corps and was beginning again. Gerber had nothing to say. He shrugged.

Morrow stopped, turned and looked back at them. "What are you two doing?"

"Nothing," answered Fetterman. When she turned and moved toward the Continental Shelf, he whispered. "It's all true. You know it and I know it."

"Well, shit," Gerber said, "I guess we'll have to do something about it."

"I guess we will," agreed Fetterman.

THE AFTERNOON WAS HOT, sticky and uncomfortable. The air seemed stagnant. It hung there, sapping the strength from everyone. Nothing moved, and the sounds from the jungle had quieted, as if the animals were also affected by the heat and humidity. There wasn't even the distant pop of rotor blades or the boom of distant artillery.

Williams sat on the wooden porch of the headquarters building, feeling as if he could get up and walk out of the camp anytime he wanted. There was no cage for him now, and no shackles hindered his movement. He was almost as free as any of the Vietnamese who sat outside. The big difference was that they all had weapons and he had none.

He raised a hand and wiped the sweat from his face, surprised at how difficult the simple action was. He had almost no strength now. The heat had gotten it. If he'd been with his unit, humping the boonies, they would have stopped for a rest. Otherwise men would have been passing out from the heat. It was too hot and humid for any strenuous activity, and at the moment, walking was a strenuous activity.

Williams heard a sound behind him and turned his head. Van stood in the doorway of the headquarters. Near him was the woman who had come to inspect Williams the night before. Now she was dressed in the green uniform of an NVA officer, though she wore no insignia that would give him a clue about her rank. Her hair hung down to her waist.

"Comrade," said Van, "this is the American. His name is Williams."

"Good afternoon, Comrade Williams," she said in heavily accented English.

Williams nodded, then stood up, moving slowly. "Good afternoon."

Van smiled. "I'll leave you two to get acquainted while I make my rounds." He moved to the steps, descended and walked off across the compound.

Williams didn't know what to do. He looked up at the woman, thinking that she was prettier than most of the Vietnamese women he had seen. She was taller, with a good figure and white teeth that were pointed from chewing on sugarcane. He didn't know what to say to her. In everything that he had heard or read about captivity by an enemy, there had been nothing like this.

Nothing about being introduced to a good-looking enemy officer. He stood there dumbly.

The woman came down the steps, stopped, then sat down. She waved a hand in front of her face as if trying to fan herself. Then, grinning up at him, she opened the first button of her bright green fatigue shirt and pulled the material away from her body. Glancing up at him, she blew down the front of her shirt.

From where he stood, he could see her small breasts. Sweat dripped between them. Williams found that he couldn't pull his eyes away from the sight.

The woman didn't stop there. She looked up at him again and slowly licked her lips. Then, just as slowly, she unbuttoned the rest of her shirt and pulled the damp material away from her skin. With one hand she wiped away the sweat.

"We do not have to remain out here," she said. Williams had to listen carefully to understand her. "We can go inside."

Williams shrugged. "You're the boss."

"What?"

"We can do whatever you say."

She stood, making no move to conceal her chest from him. She let him stare at her as she climbed the steps and moved into the headquarters building. Just inside the door she stopped and turned. As Williams joined her, she pushed the door closed and shrugged her way out of her shirt, standing there in front of him, naked to the waist.

Although he found it hard to pull his eyes from her, he still noticed that the walls were wooden and that there were pictures, maps and flags hanging on them. Ho Chi Minh stared down at him from over a small, makeshift desk. There were only a few papers and a single pen on the desk. In the corner, near another door, a rifle leaned against the wall. He knew he would never get to it before she yelled a warning. Besides, he thought, it was probably unloaded. It was some kind of trick.

She moved toward him and touched him lightly, her fingers on his chest. Williams stood still, as if afraid that motion would break the spell. He was no longer a prisoner of war but a young man with a good-looking woman paying him some attention. It was the first time he could remember that a woman had started the action. She was taking the initiative, and there seemed to be no indication that she planned to stop soon. She wasn't just teasing him.

Williams felt a need to talk. He didn't want to stop her as she worked at unbuckling his pants, but he did want to talk. He had to hear the sound of a voice. Finally, almost in desperation, he asked, "What's your name?"

"Name not important," she said. Then she looked at him and added, "You can call me Miss Kitty."

For a moment Williams didn't react. And then he chuckled. "Miss Kitty? This really is becoming the Old West."

She crouched in front of him and pulled his pants down. He stood there with her kneeling in front of him, his crotch exposed now. Her fingers probed gently. He felt himself respond to her. Thinking that she was using her mouth, he looked down to find her staring up at him, her hands on him.

"You understand now?" she asked.

He reached up to unbutton his jungle jacket. "I understand completely."

Miss Kitty took charge, knowing exactly what she wanted to do. She helped him out of his jungle jacket and then watched as he stepped out of his boots and pants until he was standing naked in front of her. She didn't let him undress her. She did it herself, peeling herself out of her clothes and dropping them onto the floor. Then she stood naked in front of him, her skin glistening with sweat.

She moved toward him, kissed his chest and fingered him, gently teasing him until he was rigid. Then she knelt in front of him, kissed him for a moment and lay back, her knees bent and drawn toward her chest. ''You like?'' she asked.

Williams ignored the question. He crouched between her legs and looked down on her. Her breasts were small, but the nipples were erect, pointing up at him. There was very little hair on her, which made her look like a young girl.

''Hurry,'' she told him.

Williams did as she told him. He stretched out but kept his full weight off her. She rose to meet him and guided him with her hands, moaning quietly as he moved forward.

Finished in a few minutes, Williams rolled to the right, but Miss Kitty wasn't ready to stop. She turned and kissed his chest, belly and thighs. With her fingers and lips, she worked at him until he was ready again. Then, when he was on his back, she straddled him, leaning forward to kiss his chin and neck.

This time it was slower. She controlled it, moving rapidly until it seemed he would explode, and then slowing, resting, until he could take more movement. She kept him on the edge for almost twenty minutes. And then she pushed it too far, too fast, and Williams erupted, slamming up against her, momentarily ending the game.

They rolled apart, both soaked in mingled sweat. They lay together, separated by a few inches, both breathing rapidly. Williams thought he was going to pass out. When she touched him, he laughed and said, "It'll take a while."

She persisted for a moment, and when he didn't respond quickly, she gave up and fell asleep. He lay there quietly, listening to his own breathing and to the sounds of birds, monkeys and insects outside. There was a distant rumbling that could have been a thunderstorm, an artillery barrage or a B-52 strike. It was too far away to know for sure.

Williams watched quietly as the light slowly faded and a breeze began to blow. Not a cool breeze that brought relief, but a warm one that made the camp a little less miserable. It didn't dry the sweat on his body.

Miss Kitty woke up and looked at him. She grinned, rolled onto her side and hiked her knees up slightly. Reaching out to touch him, she asked, "You go again?"

"Not now. Not this soon."

"We eat, then?"

Now that she had mentioned it, Williams realized he was hungry. Hungry and thirsty. "We eat," he said, almost as if he expected them to hop into a car and drive down to the local restaurant.

He stood up and dressed, then watched as she climbed back into her clothes. She took her time, pulling everything on slowly as if she were doing a reverse striptease.

"You ready?" she finally asked.

"All set."

"You follow me. You do not listen to the others. They are not important."

Williams didn't understand what she meant, but then remembered he was a prisoner. He wasn't free to leave if he felt like it. Suddenly he felt cold, as if he had be-trayed his fellow soldiers. Thinking about it, he couldn't see how he had betrayed them, but the feeling was there, gnawing at him.

She moved toward him, took his hand and pulled him toward the door. "We go."

Williams pulled his hand free but nodded. "We go."

8

MACV HEADQUARTERS
SAIGON

Gerber sat in the visitor's chair, and Fetterman stood against the filing cabinets, just as they always did. Maxwell was hunched over his desk as if there were no visitors. He held a file in one hand and a can of Coke in the other.

"What we need, Jerry, is for you to get in touch with the people up in Da Nang and get us a copy of the report they prepared."

"Can't see where that will help." Maxwell dropped the file and turned to face Gerber. "Not if their information is from that area."

"Come on, Jerry," said Fetterman, "if it's the same guy, there'll be a method of operation. That might give us a clue. Maybe they identified his unit, or maybe the fact that he was there and now he's here will identify it. How do we know what we'll find until we see it?"

"You two blasted out of here acting as if you didn't believe a word I said."

Gerber shook his head. "Is that what this is all about? Did we hurt your feelings?" He glanced at Fetterman and said, "Well, we're both sorry about that, but you have to look at it from our point of view. There were only a few rumors. Nothing concrete."

"So, you believe Morrow, but you don't believe me."

"Now, Jerry," said Gerber, "you know that's not true. If the situation had been reversed, we wouldn't have believed her until you arrived with the new data. That's all."

"Okay," said Maxwell. He took a drink of his Coke and set the can down amid the snowdrift of papers. "Tell me what you want here."

"Tony?" Gerber said.

Fetterman straightened up and pushed a couple of files out of his way. "We need a better fix on this thing. If we have to search all of Three Corps, it's going to take forever. We need some information that'll cut down the search area and time."

"I would think your own Intelligence people could get you that," Maxwell said.

"And you'd be right," agreed Gerber. He stopped, rubbed his chin, then added, "But we don't want to duplicate effort. First we need to see the report and see if we can figure out why he left I Corps. Then you need to check the CIA sources and coordinate with the ARVN to see what they know about where he's hiding."

"That'll tip our hand," Maxwell objected.

"I'm not concerned with that," said Gerber. "Billy won't care. In fact, he'll probably be happy to hear he's got such a reputation, so talking to the ARVN won't compromise our position."

Maxwell shook his head and picked up a file. He opened it, scanned it and dropped it. "I'll see what's known around here."

"Any information we get on the subject will help," said Gerber. "Our original assumption is that he'll be someplace close to the border."

"All right," Maxwell concluded. "I'll see what I can do."

"Hey, Jerry," said Fetterman, "don't knock yourself out."

"Now what in hell does that mean?"

"It means," said Gerber, taking over, "that the original mission was your idea, not ours. Now that we've worked up some enthusiasm for it, you seem to have lost all your interest in it."

"I have a lot of other irons in the fire," answered Maxwell.

"Hell," said Gerber, "we can find something else to do if you don't want to help us."

"Okay," Maxwell concluded. "Okay, I'll get on it. Where will you two be?"

"Carasel," said Gerber, and rose to go.

"Oh, on that other matter," Maxwell said. "The ARVN and the gunfight this morning...?"

"Yes?" Gerber said, raising an eyebrow.

"A formal protest has been issued by the ARVN commander in the area. He claims some Americans went wild and shot up one of his units."

"So, what's going to happen?" asked Gerber.

"Nothing," replied Maxwell. "No one seems to know anything about it, and orders have gone out to the Twenty-fifth Infantry Division to see if it involved any of their people. The assumption is that it's their area of operations and therefore it must have been their people."

"What about the women?" asked Fetterman.

"I haven't heard a thing about them," said Maxwell. "If I hear anything, I'll let you know."

Gerber stepped to the door. He stopped and rubbed his chin slowly, as if deep in thought. "If Billy doesn't want to be found, it's going to be very hard for us to locate him. Damn near impossible."

"I think that's the least of our problems," said Maxwell. "He'll want to be found." As Fetterman opened the door, Maxwell looked at him and asked, "Have you given up the idea that he is ARVN?"

Fetterman shrugged. "It made a little sense before. It would be easier for an ARVN, but I think there's too much information that suggests he's NVA."

"Glad to hear that," Maxwell commented.

"If I don't hear anything from you by noon," Gerber said, "we'll be back here. If this guy's killing Americans like that, we've got to get him."

"That's what I told you before," said Maxwell.

Gerber didn't respond. He stepped into the hallway and waited for Fetterman.

"That didn't gain us much," said Fetterman.

"We've pissed him off," said Gerber, grinning. "If there's anything to be found now, he'll find it for us."

"So, while he's working his ass off, we head downtown and eat a big dinner."

"Only because it's going to be us in the field if he finds anything. That's only fair."

"Then let's go eat," said Fetterman.

WILLIAMS SAT at a small table in one corner of the mess hootch while the Vietnamese used the long tables and tried not to see him. They straggled in, were given a steaming bowl of rice and a cup of water and sat down to eat. When they finished, they got out, ignoring the American and the Vietnamese woman.

Williams was given a big dinner. There was rice, potatoes and a large steak. There was even a bottle of steak sauce. Williams didn't ask where any of it came from. He ate the food, drank the Coke he was given and pretended he was an important visitor. As he finished the steak, it hit him just what was happening. He was the condemned man being treated like a king right up until the moment of his execution.

Fear hit him in the pit of the belly. He felt his skin crawl and his balls tingle. He turned his attention to the woman, then forced himself to think about the gunfight. He had a chance. It was like walking point day after day. There was a good chance he'd get hit, that he would be killed, but he might survive, too. He'd get through it. He wouldn't make the fatal mistake that would kill him.

It would be that way with the gunfight. Van would miss on his first shot. Williams knew that was the key to winning. It wasn't that important to get off the first shot. Accuracy was what counted. It would do Van no good to fire first, not if he missed. Williams had practiced with a pistol every chance he'd gotten. He'd make his first shot count. Van would be the one who died.

Williams turned his attention to his meal, feeling better now. He wasn't the condemned man, because the condemned didn't have a fifty-fifty chance to survive. The condemned man had absolutely no chance at all.

"Is the food satisfactory?" Miss Kitty asked.

"It's very good," said Williams, feeling a little more like Marshal Dillon. "Much better than I would have expected."

"It is special," she said. "A good meal so that you will be ready for the test in the morning. It would not be fair if you were weakened by lack of food."

"I'm glad to hear that," said Williams. If Van was worried about keeping the fight fair, Williams was sure he would win. Van's concern for Williams's health suggested Van wouldn't cheat. It meant that Williams and Chavez would be back in American hands by nightfall the next day. He picked up the can of Coke, drank some, then asked, "Would you care to share this?"

"No," she said. "I am not thirsty."

"Aren't you going to eat?"

"Not now," she said. "Later. I am not hungry now."

Williams turned his attention to his meal. "I wish you'd join me."

"I will be with you all night," she said, "if that is what you desire."

"It is what I desire," Williams replied.

WHILE WILLIAMS WAS in the mess hootch with Miss Kitty, Van was in the headquarters building with Sergeant Tran. They had been in the back room, which Van used as his personal quarters. They had listened to the sounds of the lovemaking and had peeked at Williams and Miss Kitty, using the small holes in the wall. When they had tired of that, they had used another of the doors to get out of the hootch. Williams hadn't known they were there, but the woman had. Part of her performance had been to entertain the two voyeurs.

Van sat on a chair, his feet propped on the cot he used at night, while Tran sat on a bamboo mat on the floor, the pieces of a Soviet-made Mosin-Nagant sniper rifle spread out around him.

"You'll be ready in the morning, won't you?" asked Van quietly.

"I'm always ready," answered Tran, "though you've rarely needed my services."

Van grinned at the NCO. He patted the holstered pistol. "Sometimes they fool you, these Americans. Too many of them have grown up with pistols for practice and cowboy tales for inspiration. Too many of them understand gunfights."

"Not completely," corrected Tran, beginning to reassemble the rifle, now that he had cleaned the whole thing.

Van knew what Tran was saying. Most of the Americans thought that the gunfights in the Old West had been fair. Two men, or four, or eight, facing one another in the street, each man or each side the equal to the other. Van knew that it hadn't been that way for the most part. In the majority of cases, gunfights had been one-sided affairs. One man ambushed another, or one side hid a couple of riflemen somewhere to ensure victory. That lesson hadn't been lost on Van. He had incorporated it into his private gunfights. Tran was the rifleman who made sure that Van wasn't outdrawn and killed.

Tran had saved him a couple of times. The Americans, looking for an advantage, had sometimes tried to draw on the count of one instead of three. One man had been fast enough to nearly get Van, who always drew on two. If it hadn't been for Tran in the trees with the sniper rifle, Van might have lost that fight. And Tran had drilled two others who had survived the first shot by Van when he had missed them, snapping off a shot without aiming.

Tran finished putting together the rifle, then worked the bolt, making sure it operated smoothly. "What will happen to the wounded American?"

"When the gunfight is over, we'll shoot him, too. He's too ill for us to keep alive."

"Does your victim know that?"

"He's been told his friend will be cared for if he loses." Van shrugged. "What else could I tell him? If he knew the truth, he wouldn't play the game."

Tran stood up and moved to the side so that he could set the rifle down on the cot. He turned to face Van. "And I kill the man, even if he should win."

"The American doesn't walk away," said Van. "You know that. But you'd better not let him shoot me. If I get shot and don't die, you will."

Tran sat down on the cot and patted the butt of the sniper rifle. "Don't worry about that. You won't get shot under any circumstances."

Van nodded, then grinned. "I love this. It's so easy and the Americans are so dumb. They never suspect they don't have a fighting chance. That's all they want, a fighting chance."

"But you don't give it to them."

"No," said Van. "Never."

9

NEAR THUAN LOI

For Williams the night passed too quickly. Miss Kitty was agreeable to anything he wanted to try. She found him a cold beer and more Coke. She served him naked, kneeling at his feet and bowing her head, holding the sweat-beaded can up for him to take or refuse as the mood moved him.

Williams tried a lot of different things. It was the first time in his life that a woman had been willing to extend her sexual favors to him in such a blatant way. He couldn't believe his good luck.

So he allowed Miss Kitty to do anything she could think of to bring pleasure to him. She sucked him and fondled him and then rode him. He was on top, on the bottom and then on his side. They tried it in a chair, on the floor and at the desk. They faced each other, she let him enter from the rear, they tried it head to foot. There was nothing too strange that she refused to do. Anything was fine, if it pleased him.

Williams didn't realize that one of her missions was to keep him awake as long as possible. A man who had only two or three hours of sleep wouldn't be quite as quick as a man who had gotten a full eight hours. Van had thought everything through in advance.

Williams fell asleep quite late, very late, and he was awakened early by Miss Kitty. She stood over him, wearing only the shirt of her fatigues. Kneeling next to him, she touched him and asked, "Are you ready for breakfast?"

Williams tried to blink the sleep from his eyes, which burned. They felt as if someone had thrown a handful of sand into them. There was a dull pounding in his head. He hadn't gotten enough sleep on the most important day of his life. He sat up. "How soon?"

"Now. The cooks are preparing the meal. Dai Uy Van has asked that you join him."

Williams rubbed a hand over his face. He could feel his coarse beard. He needed to shave. His hair was damp with sweat from the humidity and activity of the night. He looked at the woman. "Is it a good idea to eat breakfast with the man I'm to face in a gunfight?"

"Why not? There is no real animosity between the two of you. It is something that has been forced on you by the governments that control the situation. There is no reason to hate each other."

"Except that we're enemies," said Williams.

Miss Kitty sat back. "Why are you enemies?"

"Because," Williams began, but then stopped. They were enemies because men in Washington and men in Hanoi had decided they should be. The North Vietnamese had done nothing to him until he had arrived in Vietnam. He hadn't heard of Ho Chi Minh until he had gotten his orders for Vietnam. Then, suddenly, knowing he was going to Vietnam, he'd become interested in the news reports about the war being fought there.

For an instant he was no longer in the hootch in the jungle of South Vietnam. He was back home, in the World, sitting at the dinner table while reporters on the six o'clock news told him about the war in Vietnam. His father sat at the head of the table, where he'd been for as long as Williams could remember. His mother was opposite his father, and his two younger sisters sat across from him. The family ate their dinner, ham, as he remembered. He picked up his glass of milk, took a drink, then noticed the eyes of his eldest sister. They were full of tears that finally spilled over.

"Hey," he asked her, "what's this?"

She didn't say anything. Instead, she fled the table, bumping into the wall as she tried to get out of the room too quickly.

Williams's mother put down her fork. "Sheila's a little upset by all this Vietnam nonsense. She's been reading the newspapers and watching the television news. She's very worried about you."

"Maybe I should go talk to her," suggested Williams.

"No," said her mother. "Finish your dinner. I'll go see her."

Sitting in the hootch in Vietnam now, he remembered telling his parents and his sisters that he wouldn't be involved in anything dangerous. Trained as a clerk-typist, he had told them he'd be working in an office where the most dangerous thing would be to get his fingers stuck between the keys of his typewriter. They'd all laughed, but no one had believed him.

Just before he had left, his father had taken him aside and said, "I never told anyone this before, but I was on Guadalcanal as a Marine clerk-typist, only they gave me a rifle and I spent months defending that hellhole of an island from the Japanese.''

Williams had shrugged and said, ''I'm not really a clerk-typist.''

''I know, son. You be very careful. It'd kill your mother if anything should happen to you.''

''Nothing's going to happen,'' Williams had said.

But now it seemed that something *was* going to happen. He was already reported as missing in action. If his luck didn't hold, he'd soon be killed in action and the premonition that Sheila had had at the dinner table would come true.

''We should go,'' said Miss Kitty.

Williams got to his feet, then turned and faced the window. It was still dark out. There was a glow from one of the hootches, an orange glow that filtered out of the window and lit the ground around it. Williams couldn't see anything else.

Miss Kitty stood and pulled on her pants. She slipped her feet into her Ho Chi Minh sandals, then moved to Williams, taking his hand and gently pulling him toward the door.

They left the hootch, walked across the camp and entered the mess hall. Van was sitting at a small table. He was no longer wearing his uniform. Now he wore a western-style shirt with a fringe on it, blue jeans and cowboy boots. A leather cowboy holster rode low on his hips. His Stetson sat on the table next to him. ''Good morning,'' he said.

''Morning,'' said Williams. He was pushed toward the table, and as he approached it, another Vietnamese man pulled out a chair, indicating that Williams should sit there. As he sat down, Miss Kitty disappeared but then returned, carrying a bowl of rice. She set it in front of Williams, pulled out another chair and sat down.

Van pointed at the bowl. "Eat."

"Is there any coffee?" asked Williams.

"Tea," said Miss Kitty. "We have some tea, but we have no coffee."

Williams nodded, then picked up a spoon. He took a bit of rice, chewed and swallowed. Miss Kitty got up, walked to the left and came back with the tea. Williams drank some of it, then shook his head. "Not the same as coffee."

Van ate his rice without another word. He nodded at Miss Kitty and grinned at her, but he didn't speak. When he finished, he sat back and waited as Williams drank his tea. The American hardly touched his rice.

"What time are we going to do this?" Williams asked finally.

Van shrugged. "This morning. When it's light enough to see easily. When we're ready."

"I'd like to see Chavez before we do it," said Williams.

"Your friend spent a quiet night. He's resting. I've had the medic look in on him several times."

"Can he travel?"

Van laughed. "Pretty sure of yourself, aren't you?"

"Just planning ahead. I'm sure your men will be less than thrilled with me. I figure it's best if we get out as quickly as possible."

"Your friend Chavez might need some assistance to travel, but should you win, that assistance will be provided by my soldiers."

Williams pushed away the rice and finished his tea. "I'm ready."

"Patience," said Van. "There are a few preliminaries for us to take care of first, then we'll get to it."

Miss Kitty stood up. "Please come with me, if you've finished eating."

Standing, Williams said, "I'm all done."

They returned to the hootch, but this time Miss Kitty didn't shed her clothes. Instead, she sat behind the desk and watched Williams. He glanced at her, then began to pace up and down, stopping occasionally to look out the window, waiting for the gunfight to start.

The sun came up, and the jungle around them brightened. Now the hootches, the men, everything was visible from the window. It was all wrapped in a dim green glow as sunlight filtered down through the triple canopy.

"How soon?" asked Williams finally. "How soon until we get moving?"

"When he's ready," she said. "Sit down. You're going to wear yourself out."

"Shit," said Williams, but he turned from the window and pulled out one of the flimsy chairs. He studied the walls, the North Vietnamese flag, the battle maps and the picture of Ho Chi Minh.

"It will not help to worry," she told him.

"Won't hurt," said Williams. He tried to take his mind off the gunfight, but all he could see was Clint Eastwood facing Lee Van Cleef in a small circle in the center of a graveyard. Close-ups of the faces and the hands and the guns as the music built until one of them drew. One man down on the ground, groaning and bleeding while the other filled him with lead. And then he thought of the hangings in that movie. He couldn't remember the name of it. Eastwood in the distance, cutting the rope so that his partner could escape. The situation suggested something to him. Van might have a partner in the trees as insurance. He whirled toward Miss Kitty. "Is this going to be a fair fight?"

"What do you mean?"

"Is there anyone hidden with a rifle, just in case I might be a little too fast?"

She stood and came toward him, fastening herself to him and rubbing his crotch. "Of course it will be fair. There would be no challenge if it was not."

"Are you sure?"

"The orders have already been given, in case you should win the fight."

Williams peeled himself away from her and returned to the window. The circle was still bare, but the bleachers were filling up with men. They straggled in, sat down and waited patiently. "Why do we have to wait so long? Let's just get it done."

The door opened then, and Van stood there, easily the shortest cowboy who ever lived. He wore his black-Stetson now, pushed back on his head, the definitive drugstore cowboy. One hand rested on the butt of his revolver. "You ready?"

"I don't have a weapon," said Williams.

Van turned and snapped his fingers. Another man entered, carrying a second gun belt. Van pointed at it. "That's your revolver."

Williams moved forward and took the gun belt from the man. He drew the weapon from the holster.

"There are only two rounds in it," said Van. He grinned. "I'm sure you understand."

Holstering the gun, Williams put the belt around his waist. He buckled it, adjusted it and pushed it down slightly. Then he drew the revolver again, holstered it and tied the leather thong around his leg.

"If you're ready," said Van.

"Chavez?" Williams asked.

"Is resting comfortably. He drank some tea this morning and then went back to sleep."

Williams drew the gun again. It slipped from the holster smoothly. He thumbed back the hammer of the single-action weapon, then let it down slowly. He noticed the cylinder spun counterclockwise. Checking the load, he set it so that cocking the revolver again would put the first of the two rounds under the hammer. "I'm ready now."

"Then let's go." Van turned and stepped out of the hootch onto the porch.

Williams hesitated, glanced at Miss Kitty, then said, "Thank you for making this last night one to remember."

She nodded but didn't say a word to him. Instead, she stood up and preceded him out the door. As she passed Williams, she stared straight ahead, as if he no longer existed.

Williams followed Van out into the humid morning air. Sweat beaded immediately. He wiped his hand on the front of his jungle fatigues. The last thing he wanted was a palm slippery with sweat, especially when his life depended on quickness.

Van stepped over the low wall of the circle and took up a position on the northern side, facing south. The bleachers holding the spectators were to his left.

Now Williams took up his position just inside the circle, twenty feet from Van. He stared at the smaller man, focusing on his eyes. There didn't seem to be any fear in Van's face. It was as if the North Vietnamese officer was standing in front of a class of recruits about to lecture them on the importance of firearm safety.

"One of the men will count to three," said Van. "At three we draw and fire. The man left standing will be the winner. If you win, you, along with your Comrade Chavez, can leave this camp. If you lose, you'll be buried in the jungle. Do you have any questions?"

"What will happen to Chavez if I lose?" Williams asked again.

"He'll be cared for, and if he survives, he'll become a prisoner of war."

"Let's get it done," said Williams.

Van nodded, turned to his men and said in Vietnamese, "If the American wins, he, along with his friend, is free to go. I want that understood." Finished with his speech, Van again faced Williams. "It is now time." He reached down and unhooked the leather thong looped over the hammer of his pistol. Wiping a hand on his chest, he stared into Williams's eyes. He hesitated and finally nodded.

"One," said Miss Kitty.

Williams flexed his fingers, then wiped his other hand over his mouth. The image of Lee Van Cleef facing Clint Eastwood sprang into his mind, and he forced it out. He had to concentrate on Van.

"Two," said Miss Kitty.

And as he had always done in the past, Van drew. But Williams had been ready for that. Had expected it. He drew at the same time, the revolver coming out of his holster easily. He pulled back the hammer and knew that he had won. Van hadn't cleared his holster. His weapon was still pointed at the ground. Williams felt a grin spread over his face.

The bullet took Williams from the rear. He felt the pain explode in his back, a white-hot blaze that felt like a poker rammed into his flesh. He tried to fire his gun, but he couldn't see the target. He didn't know if he was standing or if he was still in the circle. He fired once, but the round struck the top of the low stone wall and ricocheted up into the bleachers. A man screamed in sudden pain and surprise and toppled from his seat.

Now Van got into the act. Standing with his right side facing Williams, he fired once. The round hit Williams in the chest, driving him back. He fell, rolled and lost the grip on his revolver.

Van walked toward the American and looked down. Blood had spattered the front of his fatigues. It was spreading in a crimson stain across his belly. There was no intelligence left in his eyes. Williams had died as he had hit the ground.

Van whirled and looked at the men in the bleachers and those crouched around the body of the man wounded by Williams's single, wild shot.

"He's dead!" yelled a man.

Van turned and watched Tran coming out of the jungle. "You were a little slow."

"I covered you," said Tran.

Van hooked a thumb over his shoulder at the crowd of men. "His one shot killed one of ours."

"Unfortunate," said Tran. "Do you want me to take care of the other American?"

Van looked down at Williams. The blood was pooling under him, making it look as if he were floating in it. Flies were gathering already. "No," he said. "That's a job I've saved for myself."

"Are we going to bury them in the jungle?"

"The one called Chavez, yes. This one I want to dump at the gate to their closest camp. Give them all something to think about in the future."

Tran studied the body of the dead American. "That was close," he said.

"Closer than it should have been." He looked up at Tran. "I'll just have to be faster next time."

10

MACV-SOG BUILDING
TAN SON NHUT

Gerber sat at the table in the planning room of the SOG building, studying the maps that Kepler had supplied. Fetterman sat opposite him, sipping a Coke, and Kepler stood near the door, waiting to answer any questions.

"I can't see anything that looks likely," said Gerber, finally sitting back. He pointed at the maps. "Lots of enemy activity in and around Dong Xoai, but nothing that gives us any clues."

Kepler, his arms folded across his chest, said, "I've received a report about a platoon ambushed in the area around there in the past couple of days."

Gerber looked at the intel NCO. "You get anything else?"

"Yes, sir. Seems three or four men are missing. They, meaning the parent unit, only recently discovered the ambush site and are trying to put together an accurate picture. That means the details are sketchy, but they do know that a few men are missing."

Gerber leaned over the map. "That's in the area we were searching."

"Yes, sir. I've talked to my agents there again, but I'm getting nothing of value. If your friend Billy the Zip's working the area, he's at a camp that was established before he got there. There are no rumors of anything new."

"Then there's nothing for us to go on. No place for us to begin the search."

Kepler moved from the door to the table. He glanced at the map. "If you really want a place to start a search, then I'd suggest somewhere out in the Dong Xoai area. North, toward the mountains."

"Except that we've got some problems with the ARVN out there."

"Captain," said Fetterman, interrupting for the first time. "You know as well as I do that we could pinpoint Billy's hiding place within a square mile and still spend the rest of our lives searching for him."

Gerber nodded. "Hell, we could walk over top of him and never know it."

"So our searching probably isn't going to do us any good," said Fetterman.

"There a point to this, Tony?"

"Yes, sir. If we assume our Billy the Zip is the same guy Robin found out about up north, we know he has a tremendous ego. He's the fastest gun in the East. Goes up against armed men and outdraws them all."

"Granted."

"Then the way to smoke him out is to start rumors of an American who's faster than anyone, East or West. Start rumors about someone who can't be beat by anyone. When Billy hears it, he's going to start looking for that man. He's going to want to face him, which saves us all the trouble of searching for the guy.''

"And who's going to be the fastest gun in the East or West?'' asked Gerber.

"Since it was my idea,'' said Fetterman, grinning broadly, "it's only fair that I get the reputation.''

"Not so, Master Sergeant,'' said Gerber. "I think my younger age makes me the logical choice. I'm quicker than you, I outrank you and I can take him.''

"Age makes no difference,'' said Fetterman.

"How many forty-year-old baseball players do you see? Everyone slows down.''

"Captain, age doesn't do it. The old players have learned the game so well that quickness isn't as important as it was. Older players get out of the game because they want to move beyond being on the field. They're looking for more in their lives than just chasing a little ball around. They've matured, but that doesn't mean they're no longer able to play. They replace quickness with understanding, and if they retain the quickness, then they're even better.''

Gerber reached across the table and picked up Fetterman's Coke. He drank some of it and set it down. "I think I should be the one to go up against Billy.''

"No, sir. I think it should be me. I'm wise to the ways of his kind. I know what to look for.''

"What do you mean, his kind?'' asked Gerber.

"He cheats,'' said Fetterman.

"How do you know?''

"Because people like that always cheat. He'll draw a moment too soon. He'll stand so that you're facing the sun. He'll do little things that'll give him the advantage. I'll be ready for that.''

Kepler stepped in. "Instead of arguing about it, why don't you two just flip a coin?"

Gerber laughed. "Because I don't have a coin."

Kepler pulled one out of his pocket, flipped and said, "Call it in the air."

"Heads," said Gerber.

"Tails," said Kepler, who then grinned at Fetterman. "Looks like it's your job."

"I'm not going to be railroaded into this," Gerber objected, glaring at Kepler.

"I've won the toss fair and square," said Fetterman.

"We'll see how things develop," said Gerber. "If it works out right, you can face Billy. But we'll just have to wait and see." In the back of his mind he could see ways to prevent such an event from happening. At the moment it wasn't worth discussing, because they weren't even sure they would be able to locate Billy.

"So, what are you going to do?" asked Kepler.

"I think," said Gerber, "that we'll find ourselves a couple of good revolvers and practice with them. Get good at what the Army now calls the quick kill. Point and shoot without ever aiming at the target."

"And how are you going to promote this thing so that Billy comes looking for you?" asked Kepler.

"We'll get Robin to help us there," said Gerber. "Oh, and we'll let things drop within earshot of our ARVN allies. Won't be hard to find someone to carry the tale back to Billy. Then it's up to him."

"I can think of about a dozen ways this can blow up in your face," said Kepler.

"Of course," said Gerber. "What's new?"

HAVING WON THE GUNFIGHT, barely, and only because Tran had been hiding in the trees with his sniper rifle,

Van was still feeling good. Exhilarated. He needed a woman badly. Immediately. And the only woman around was Miss Kitty, the very woman who had spent the night with Williams, trying to slow him down. Van decided he didn't care.

Leaving Williams where he had fallen, Van stormed across the circle, stepped over the wall and grabbed Miss Kitty by the wrist. "You come with me."

She didn't say anything. She turned to follow, stumbled but didn't fall. She had known what would happen next. Van often reacted to a fight this way. It didn't matter if he won fairly, as he often did, or if he had to cheat, as had been the case with Williams. Either way he was still wound up from it. There was an edge that he couldn't take off easily. It was the anticipation of the event. A week of planning it, a couple of days of playing with the victim, almost like a cat playing with a cornered mouse, and then the final, climactic fight. Van needed something to help him come down from it all. He needed a woman.

He almost leaped up the steps to the porch of the headquarters, kicked open the door and pushed the woman inside. Slamming the door, he forced her to the rear of the room, through the doorway and back into his quarters. He was right behind her, breathing down her neck. "Strip," he ordered.

"If I don't want to?" she asked meekly.

Van stopped and looked at her. "You've never refused me before."

"I'm not refusing," she said. "I was asking a question. What if I don't want to?"

Van sat down on his cot and pulled off his boots, tossing them onto the floor. He unbuckled his gun belt and dropped it near him. When he looked up and saw that she hadn't moved, he said, "I'm not in the mood for any games now." He stared at her until she started to unbutton her fatigue shirt quickly.

When he finished undressing, he stood up and waited. He moved to her, wanting to help her, hurry her along, but didn't touch her. Instead, he stood there, shaking with impatience and anticipation.

Finally she was naked. He grabbed her by the shoulders and pushed her around, backing her up until the backs of her legs touched the cot. She sat down and then rolled back, twisting around and stretching out.

Van joined her, but she wasn't as receptive as she had been in the past. She lay there, her legs locked together, one arm over her breasts.

"What is it?" he asked.

"You could show a little kindness," she said.

Van laughed, then forced her arm out of the way so that he could grab her right breast, squeezing it hard. "You want kindness?"

"It was just a thought," she said as she squirmed. When she was free of his grasp, she spread her legs. "If you're going to do it, hurry up and do it."

Van did as he was told, slamming his body against hers as if the physical force would create the release. He pumped away, faster and faster, until he stiffened. He plunged down, deeper, and then grabbed at her bony shoulders, grunting and biting her.

Finished, he rolled to the side, his breath rasping in his throat. He wiped the sweat from his face, then looked over at the woman. "Are you happy?"

"I'm fine," she said. She was familiar with this, too: Van taking her as fast as he could, getting the release he needed to come down from the high of having killed a man, then worrying about her. But there was never real concern in his voice. It was as if he had read something about being worried about his subordinates. He didn't care, but thought he should ask her how she felt.

Van crawled over her and stood up. He grabbed a fatigue shirt from a hook and slipped it on. Picking up his pants, he said, "I've got to get out of here. There are things that have to be done."

She didn't care. She wanted him out now, as quickly as he could get out. She turned over on her side and stared at the thatched wall.

Van finished dressing, slipped on his sandals, then picked up his revolver, leaving the holster behind. He left the room and then the headquarters, finding Tran sitting on the stone wall of the circle, staring at the body of the dead American.

As Van approached, Tran turned and said, "They've removed Sergeant Kai. Some of them are preparing to take him back to his home in the North."

"Good," said Van. He looked at his weapon—a silver revolver with an eight-inch barrel. There were grips with notches cut in them for each man he had killed in a gunfight. He was honest with the notches. If Tran shot the man, then Van didn't add to the tally. They would talk about the number of men killed in the game, but that number was higher than the number of notches. Van recorded only his kills on his pistol.

"Let's take care of the other American."

"Why waste a bullet?" asked Tran. "He'll die soon enough, anyway."

Van opened the revolver and spun the cylinder. He flipped the spent cartridges from the weapon, but then realized that without his holster he had nothing with which to replace them. He closed the weapon again, spinning the cylinder so that an empty chamber was under the hammer and the first one up would be the first of the live rounds.

"Let's go," he said.

Together the men walked across the compound to the hut where Chavez lay. Tran stepped inside and Van followed. Chavez was on his back, his ripped jungle jacket covering part of his chest and stomach. He was bathed in sweat that had turned his uniform black. He moaned quietly once, and his eyes flickered open and then closed again.

For a moment Van looked down on the helpless man, feeling compassion for him. Here was a soldier who had been wounded in battle. He had fought bravely and been injured in that fight. He had been carried from the field, and Van had hoped he would be easy to help. A bandage, a few pills, and he would have another victim for his gunfighting adventures. Chavez was hurt too badly for that. The only thing Van could do was kill the man quickly and get it over with.

"Want me to do it?" asked Tran.

"No. This one's mine." He raised his gun and aimed at the center of Chavez's face. He saw the sickly color of the skin, the beads of sweat on it, the streaks of dirt and dried blood. Slowly Van squeezed the trigger, letting the weapon fire itself. The bullet slammed into Chavez with a wet smack and a snap of breaking bone. The man's eyes bulged with shock. A bloodless third eye appeared as the back of Chavez's head blew off in a spray of blood, brain and bone. Blood suddenly spurted through the small bullet hole above his right eye. He spasmed, kicked, and his heels dug into the rough wood of the floor as he tried to lift himself up. Although dead already, part of his brain was still functioning, sending conflicting orders to the muscles, causing Chavez to drum his feet and to try to lift himself.

Van cocked the revolver again, but didn't shoot. Chavez seemed to collapse suddenly and was still. For a moment Van stared down at the body, then kicked it once to see whether there was any response. Satisfying himself that Chavez was dead, Van turned and walked out of the hut. He knew he should feel something about the death of a fellow human, but he couldn't. Chavez was the enemy, come to Vietnam to kill him and his comrades. It was only fitting that Chavez die instead. If Van was in California, or anywhere else in the United States, he would expect Chavez to treat him in the same way. It was the fortunes of war and the law of the jungle.

Outside, in the muggy heat of late morning, he said, "Get the garbage out of there. Bury it in the jungle and let it feed the trees."

"And the other man?"

"We'll take him back to his fellow GIs," said Van, "with a number pinned to his shirt announcing our victory over him. Let them try to figure it out."

"Very good," said Tran.

11

MACV HEADQUARTERS
SAIGON

Gerber, along with Fetterman, stood at the iron gate in the bowels of the MACV building, waiting for the MP to open it. He made them sign out first on an access roster on a clipboard and then, satisfied that neither of them was trying to sneak classified material out, opened the gate. Once they were through, he shut the gate with a loud, metallic clank that seemed to reverberate throughout the building.

Climbing the stairs that led up to the ground floor, Fetterman leaned close. "Can't believe the ARVN put a price on Billy's head."

Gerber nodded. "Billy will love it. If he's as impressed with the Old West as Maxwell says, it's just the kind of thing he'll love. Maybe we ought to get some wanted posters printed up and scatter them around."

Fetterman laughed. "I like that. Might draw Billy out quicker than anything else."

They reached the top of the steps and stopped in the hallway that led out toward the double doors. Bright sunlight streamed in, but the air-conditioning in the building kept it cool inside. No high humidity or heat to bother the generals as they planned war strategies. Just a cool environment so they'd be able to think straight as they ordered young men out to fight and die.

As Fetterman and Gerber stood there quietly, three shapes approached the double doors. One man ran forward, grabbed the handle and whipped open the door. The middle man stepped inside, and as he did, the last man rushed around to open the next door. A general entered the building.

He was a tall, slender man with an impressive mane of white hair. It was off his ears and was swept back and neatly groomed, as regulations demanded, but it wasn't short. It was long and thick and snowy white. The general seemed to be telling everyone that he might be older than most of his soldiers, but he still had all of his hair. Every single strand of it.

His uniform, regular jungle fatigue issue, was perfectly tailored. It was heavily starched with not even a thread out of place. There were no sweat stains on it. He had rolled the sleeves up so that they were halfway between the elbows and shoulders, as regulations dictated.

Fetterman touched Gerber on the shoulder, then pointed at the general's hip. He was wearing a highly polished black cowboy gun belt. There was a pearl-handled revolver in the holster, held in place by a small leather thong that slipped over the hammer.

"Billy would come out of North Vietnam for a weapon like that," said Fetterman.

"If he knew anyone had it."

"We could make sure he did. We could ask the general if we can borrow it for the mission. Then we could let everyone see it. Someone would eventually tell Billy."

Gerber laughed. "Generals don't loan their weapons to old Special Forces troopers like us."

"Wouldn't hurt to ask," said Fetterman.

The general had turned down the hall, walking toward the end of the building where all the generals had their offices, an area of mahogany doors, posh carpeting and a more pleasant shade of green paint.

Gerber moved off, trailing the general, walking faster to catch up with him. As he approached, he said, "General, might I have a word with you?"

The general stopped and turned. He looked at Gerber, whose fatigues were wrinkled, sweat-stained and bore no insignia. "Who are you?"

"Gerber, MacKenzie K., Captain. Army Special Forces." He glanced at Fetterman and added, "This is Master Sergeant Anthony B. Fetterman."

"I'm very busy," said the general. He didn't even look at Fetterman.

One of the general's aides stepped forward. "If you'd like to make an appointment, I can accommodate you."

Gerber ignored him. "General, Sergeant Fetterman and I are on a special mission, and that revolver of yours is something we could use."

The general looked at Gerber, then at his gun. "I'm afraid I don't understand."

"It's hard to explain without violating security, but your weapon could become an important part of our mission. Make it simpler on us."

"I'm sorry, Captain, but I don't see it your way. Just forget it." He turned to go.

"General, it could make our job a little easier."

"There are no circumstances where a single-action six-shooter would be more valuable than any of the weapons in the Army arsenal." He started to walk off.

Gerber glanced at Fetterman, then played his trump card. "It could save a few American lives."

Again the general stopped and faced Gerber. "There's no way my personal weapon could save any American lives." He whirled and walked off.

Gerber watched him as he disappeared into his office. "I told you he wouldn't let us borrow it."

"Which means we'll have to steal it." Fetterman said, grinning.

Gerber shot a glance at Fetterman, a look of alarm on his face. Then he grinned, too. "I guess we will."

VAN PASSED THE AFTERNOON in his headquarters, sitting behind his desk and staring out the window. At the edge of the jungle four men worked at digging a grave for Spec Four Tomás Chavez. They had learned that a grave had to be deep, not to protect the body from the jungle scavengers that sometimes dug up the dead, but to protect themselves from the odor of decay. They didn't know that burying it deep also protected them from disease.

They chopped away at the ground, cutting through the roots that made it difficult to dig. Carrying out the detail in relays, two men working and two men watching, they switched frequently, stopping when the bottom of the hole began to get wet. Jumping out, they rolled Chavez in and began throwing the dirt back in, covering him.

Miss Kitty appeared in the doorway behind Van. "Are you going out with the patrol tonight?"

Van turned his attention away from the window. "Of course. We'll be leaving soon."

"I'll go, too."

"No reason for that," said Van.

Tran entered and announced, "We're ready to go, Comrade."

"So soon?"

"We have a long way to travel to dispose of Williams. It won't be easy."

Van turned and picked up the gun belt hanging on the chair behind him. As he buckled it on, he said, "I'll be there in a few minutes."

Tran nodded and turned, leaving without another word.

"I wish to go," Miss Kitty said again.

"Then get your gear and meet us near the mess hut quickly. If you're not there, we'll leave without you. Understand?"

"Certainly."

She fled through the rear door. Van used the front, stepping out into the gloom of the jungle environment. An odor of woodsmoke hung in the air and there was no breeze at all. It was quiet all around him except for the perpetual buzz of insects.

He crossed the camp and came to the patrol, which was lined up next to Williams's body. The corpse was wrapped in a poncho liner and tied to a pole for transport. Flies swarmed around the body.

The men were dressed in black pajamas, had chest pouches with spare magazines for their weapons and had round metal canteens slung over their shoulders. Rather than wearing Ho Chi Minh sandals, each man wore small boots, modeled after the combat boot worn by French paras a decade earlier, that looked like high-topped tennis shoes.

Tran waited at one end of the group. When Van was close, he said, "We're ready."

Van hesitated, then pulled a small map from the pocket of his fatigue shirt. Like so much they had gathered, it was old and out of date, but it was the only one they had. Tran pointed to a camp at the center of the map. "A four-hour hike," he said. "We get there about dusk. Wait and then leave the body. Good cover all around."

"It's an ARVN camp," Van pointed out.

"But there are Americans there. Maybe fifty or more. It's the best place to take the body."

"Please lead the way," said Van. He glanced to the rear, but Miss Kitty hadn't appeared yet.

Tran turned to face the men. Altogether there were nineteen. Each of these men had watched the gunfight and all had seen Williams kill their friend. Tran had explained to them that dropping the body at the front gate of an American camp would scare the Americans. It was a way to get even with the enemy. Each man had eagerly agreed to transport the body to the camp.

Tran turned and walked toward the jungle. He stepped over a fallen log and into the denser vegetation. It was like moving from the manicured lawns of a park into the surrounding forest. The canopy overhead didn't change. It was as thick and heavy as it was everywhere. An occasional shaft of sunlight punched through, the rays obvious in the moisture-laden air.

Tran moved slowly, remembering that some of the men had to bear the extra weight of the dead American. He picked his way through the jungle, avoiding the thickest undergrowth, sliding through it silently, carefully, remembering that some Americans looked for the paths the enemy used. Some Americans could spot a broken branch or the disturbed carpet of rotting vegetation. They knew how to track an enemy, and Tran didn't want them finding their way back to his camp.

They walked up a gentle slope, reached the top, stopped, then started down. The canopy thinned slightly. More sun bled through it. They avoided those areas, remaining in the thick, dark shadows of the jungle, using it to conceal their movements.

They kept moving, not stopping to rest as an American unit would. They pushed on across a narrow stream and through a thicket that tore at their uniforms and skin. Thorns ripped at them, but no one said a word.

After a couple of hours they came to a clearing nearly a kilometer across. Sunlight blazed into it. Elephant grass, three feet high, covered the field. Near the center was a single, huge bomb crater.

"We cross?" asked Tran.

At first Van was tempted. It would cut their travel time and the exposure would be short. But they had the body of a dead American, and if they were caught in the open with that, every one of them would be killed. "Go around," said Van.

"Certainly."

They skirted the edge of the clearing, staying away from the sunlight. On the other side they turned, moving deeper into the jungle along the side of a ridge line, staying away from its crest.

Finally they came down off the hill and walked through a narrow valley that eventually opened up into a broader plain. In the distance, half a kilometer away, they could see the ring that formed the perimeter of the ARVN camp. There were bunkers constructed of dark green sandbags and thick timbers. A narrow road, choked by red dust, led from the small village to the camp.

"There," said Tran, pointing.

Van stood next to the thick trunk of a tree, looking out at the camp, wishing he had binoculars. There was movement in the camp, behind the bunkers, where the men thought they were safe from snipers and mortars. Near the middle of the camp was a huge bunker, the top festooned with radio antennae. It was the perfect target for a mortar or rocket squad. There was even a large white square painted on its side.

The sun was now close to the horizon. Shadows crept toward the east, stretching out and concealing some of the camp. While Van stood there, watching, lights began to appear in the camp—electric lights, accompanied by the whine of a generator.

"How soon?" asked Tran.

"When it's dark and the lights are out. When everyone's asleep," he said.

IT BOTHERED FETTERMAN all through dinner. It bothered him that a general wouldn't give up his personal weapon for a few days, even if such an action might save some American lives. It bothered him that the general had looked at him as if he were some kind of mess a dog had made on the rug. It bothered him that the general, though introduced to him, hadn't bothered to acknowledge his existence.

"That revolver's the perfect bait," he said when he and Gerber were eating their salads.

"That revolver would draw Billy out of hiding," he said while eating his main course.

"Maybe we should just go get it," he said over coffee as they listened to the quiet music playing in the background. "Tonight."

"The general isn't going to leave it lying around for us to steal," said Gerber. "And if he did, and we swiped it, he'd know it was us."

"But he wouldn't be able to prove it," said Fetterman. "That's the important thing."

Gerber agreed, and after they paid for their dinner, they stepped out into the sultry heat of the early evening. The sun had set, but the heat hadn't broken. It seemed hotter than it had been during the day. The buildings radiated the heat back at them. The pace of the city had slowed, as if its strength had been sapped.

They walked along, ignoring everything around them. Ignoring the American youngsters in ugly civilian clothes who were trying to put the make on Vietnamese girls who only wanted their money. Ignoring the pounding music and the slimy Vietnamese hucksters who were trying to drag them into a club or sell them the latest in watches or radios or tape recorders.

When they came to their jeep, Fetterman climbed behind the wheel and said, "Surely he wouldn't leave it in his office overnight."

"Probably not," agreed Gerber, "but we don't know where he's quartered. There might be a clue there. He'd have the pistol with him."

"So, we're on our way to MACV?"

"To begin."

Fetterman started the engine, waited for a break in the traffic and pulled out into the flow. They drove along in silence, letting the night wash over them. Saigon at night was bright with lights from the streets, the bars and the windows of houses. And if that wasn't enough, flares usually hung over the city, adding to the brilliance. Their bright green-yellow glare added an unreal quality to Saigon, making it look like a futuristic city at the edge of forever, a strange place where people in transition stopped for a few weeks or months or maybe a year. It was a city without real substance; by morning it could be gone.

Fetterman pulled into the MACV parking lot, which still contained cars and jeeps. There were bright lights up on poles, giving the lot and building the semblance of a large shopping mall. As he locked up the wheel, Fetterman asked, "Do you remember the man's name?"

"Nope," said Gerber. "He didn't give it and he wasn't wearing a name tag."

"So, how do we do this?"

"I think I know which office he went in. We'll search it and see what we can turn up."

For a moment Fetterman didn't move. Finally he glanced at Gerber. "This is more than a little strange. To fight this war we've got to break into a general's office and steal his unique revolver."

"No one ever said it was going to be easy."

They got out and walked up to the building. Many of the windows were still lit. The night watch was on duty, fighting the war in air-conditioned comfort. They entered the building and walked down the hallway until they came to the generals' area.

"Wish I'd brought my little burglar's kit," said Fetterman, "in case we have to pick a lock."

"Don't worry about it."

They reached a door with a brass plaque on it, announcing, Major General William Hammond.

"This is it," said Gerber. He reached down, grabbed the knob and twisted. When it turned in his hand, he smiled at Fetterman and opened the door.

The office was dark. They slipped in and closed the door. Fetterman searched for the light switch, turned it on and studied the interior. It was just like the outer office of every other general in South Vietnam. Two big desks were covered with papers, one desk for the aide and one for the secretary. A couch sat along one wall, with a coffee table, holding pristine copies of all the latest stateside magazines, in front of it.

Gerber moved to the aide's desk and glanced at the unclassified reports, letters and requests on it. There was also an appointment book, which should have been locked up. If a VC assassination squad had targeted the general, they would have his appointments for the next week or ten days for their planning purposes.

Fetterman moved across the office and tried the next door. It opened, too. He stepped in, turned on the light and looked around. "Nothing in here. No sign of any weapon."

Gerber sat down at the aide's desk and pawed through the papers. "Got it. Our general's staying at the Continental. Just like the correspondents and the embassy staff."

Fetterman looked in at him. "You got a room number?"

"Better," said Gerber. "I've got a key."

Fetterman turned off the light in the inner office. "Let's go, then."

12

OUTSIDE THE ARVN/ AMERICAN CAMP AT DONG XOAI

When the sun set, Van and his men crept out of the jungle and into the tall grass that surrounded the American base. Each man moved slowly, crawling forward carefully. It took four men to move the body, maneuvering the pole among them, lifting and pushing and trying not to rise up so that they could be seen or to make any noise that would alert the enemy.

Van, Tran and the remainder of the squad fanned out, slipping forward slowly as security. It was slow, hot work, even after the sun had gone down, but the men had done it before. After an hour and a half, they had moved only a hundred meters. The jungle was nothing more than a black smudge on the horizon behind them, while the camp was a gray blob in front of them, except for a couple of pillars of light that illuminated the bottoms of the low-hanging clouds rolling in from Cambodia.

The burst of fire caught Van by surprise. Without thinking, he flattened himself against the tough grass.

He listened to the shots being fired, then realized the Americans weren't firing at him. The gunfire definitely sounded like six-guns from the Old West.

Rising slowly so that he could see into the camp, he heard voices, Americans talking in the distant, amplified way of movie theaters. Then he saw shadows on the side of the commo bunker in the center of the camp. The Americans were watching a movie.

Twisting around and creeping forward, he managed to get into position so that he could look at the makeshift screen. Now he could see the men, dressed in black and wearing hats, facing other men in a dusty street. He was pretty certain he was looking at the Earps, Doc Holliday and the Clantons. He lifted a hand and touched his lips. Then he waved at his men, signaling them to hold where they were.

Van didn't recognize the movie, but he recognized the O.K. Corral. He waited as the gunfire began again. Men stood in the street, blazing away at one another. An Earp fell, a bullet in the leg. Another took a shot in the shoulder. Holliday fired his shotgun, and one of the Clantons dropped. Another drew and was shot down, dying in the street. A few more shots were fired, and then Ike Clanton appeared, his coat held wide open to show he wasn't armed.

Tran slipped forward and whispered, ''What's happening?''

Van tore his eyes away from the screen in the American camp. He stared into the dark face of Tran. ''There was movement in their bunkers.''

''And now?''

Van turned back. Now the celluloid men had gotten out of the street. The gunfight was over. He wondered just how heavily guarded the camp was. There were only a few Americans. The remainder of the soldiers were ARVN who would probably run if there was an attack. In the confusion he might be able to sneak in, steal the movie and get out.

Tran slipped forward and peered through the grass. "I can't see anything now."

"Relax," said Van. He looked at the bunker line and then to the rear, where his men waited. A few men could get in and out without much trouble. There had been raids by sappers on American camps in the past. Twenty men could blow a hole in the bunker line and sprint through with ease. They could even blow up a helicopter, an airplane or a bunker.

But all Van wanted to do was steal a movie. Then he'd need a projector and electricity, and if the projector broke or the film broke, that would be the end of it. No, he decided, it wasn't worth the risk.

"We've got to get going," urged Tran.

Van nodded. He glanced at the distant screen. He could see two men in a buggy. He had no idea what was happening now. The gunfight was over. "Let's move around toward the road and get the body ready," he told Tran.

The sergeant nodded and slipped away, disappearing into the dark. Van took a final look at the screen, which was now showing high mountain scenery, and then followed Tran. He came to the majority of his soldiers, who were crouched in a shallow ditch with the body of the dead American.

Tran leaned close and whispered, "There's a good place to leave the body about a hundred meters to the right, at the bottom of the perimeter wire."

"Go," said Van.

Tran led them off, slipping through the grass, staying low. Van followed until they came to the edge of the dirt road. The captain moved along it until he came to the edge of the perimeter wire. It was concertina filled with tanglefoot.

"Along here?" asked Tran.

"Perfect," said Van.

They waited while the rest of the men caught up to them. Then, using the grass to conceal their actions, they unwrapped Williams's body. Van wrote a number on a sheet of paper and stuck it into a pocket. Then, with the help of two of his men, he rolled the body out onto the road, where the Americans would be sure to see it in the morning.

"Now we get out?" asked Tran.

"Return to our camp," said Van. "Go."

Tran stayed low in the grass, crawling away from the American camp as the sound of the movie drifted out to them. Van looked back once, but they were now too far away and he could no longer tell what was happening on the screen.

They reached the trees quickly. There was no indication that anyone in the camp had seen anything. He stood up, turned and looked back. No movement. The lights were all out now. No one had seen the body yet.

Van found Tran and said, "Let's rest here for a few minutes and then we'll return to our camp."

"Yes, Comrade."

THERE WAS NO ONE at the Continental Hotel to stop them. Men in fatigue uniforms were seen in the lobby and the various restaurants all day and all night long. The hotel lobby was smaller than the one in the Carasel. There were some marble columns and a teak desk at the far end, where the keys were kept and where mail was delivered in boxes. Also at the far end were a couple of elevators and an elaborate staircase that led up to the second floor.

"So, what do we do now?" asked Fetterman.

Gerber glanced at his watch. It was after midnight. He'd thought things would slow down after midnight, but the lobby was choked with men and women trying to talk one another into various activities, mostly of a sexual nature. "Let's go upstairs and see what's happening."

They walked to the elevators. Fetterman pushed the button and then waited until the doors slipped open, revealing a Vietnamese woman in an abbreviated costume sitting on a small stool.

"Your floor?"

"Four," said Gerber as he stepped in.

When Fetterman joined them, she closed the doors and they started the ascent quietly. Neither said anything as they rose. They stopped and the doors opened. Fetterman exited and Gerber followed. When the doors shut again, Gerber pointed. "Down this way."

They walked down the wide hall. The Continental might have been an elegant hotel once, but no longer. The carpeting was frayed, and the walls were dirty. There was an odor in the halls, not unlike that in the older, poorer sections of Saigon, an odor of sweat, urine, vomit and mildew.

Gerber looked at the key and then the door numbers. They reached the right room and stopped. The white door was louvered to allow air to circulate. There was no light on inside. A slight flow of cool air came through, and from the interior they could hear the hum of an air conditioner.

Gerber leaned close to the door, his left ear against it as he looked at Fetterman. There was a faint noise that sounded like someone in heavy sleep. He held a thumb up, then moved away from the door so that his shadow wouldn't fall on it. Glancing up, he saw the lights in the hallway—two fixtures on the ceiling and one mounted on the wall. He pointed at them.

Fetterman nodded and moved toward the closest. Standing on his toes, he reached upward and loosened the screws around the globe that protected the electric light. He pulled it down, set it on the floor and then loosened the light bulb.

Twenty feet away Gerber did the same thing. Then he reached up under the fixture on the wall and loosened the bulb there. When their section of the corridor was dark, he moved back to the door.

Holding the key out and pointing it at the lock, he glanced at Fetterman. When the master sergeant nodded, he slipped the key in slowly, then turned it. There was a quiet click as the lock released and the door popped open an inch. With his left hand he reached out, held the door in place and pulled the key from the lock, pocketing it.

Now he was ready to enter the room. He glanced at Fetterman, who nodded. Stepping forward, he opened the door and slipped in, backing up so that he was against the wall. Fetterman entered after him, closed the door and waited. Both men let their eyes adjust to the darkness in the room.

Slowly things came into focus. A bed was pushed against one wall. There was a chair in the corner and a wardrobe against another wall. Next to it was a window, the curtains partially closed so that some light bled in through it. Off to the right was a table with two chairs around it. A nightstand held a telephone, something most hotel rooms in Saigon didn't have. A door led to the bathroom.

Gerber crouched, changing his perspective. He saw a pair of combat boots on the floor, and shoes and a briefcase partially under the bed. He didn't see any sign of a weapon, but it wouldn't be left out in the open. He just hoped the general didn't sleep with it under his pillow. It would be impossible to retrieve then.

Fetterman moved quietly, sliding along the wall. He reached the edge of the bed and looked down at the general, who didn't move. The rhythm of his breathing didn't change.

Gerber worked his way along the other wall, moving slowly, feeling his way along with his feet and hands. He didn't look at the general, afraid that staring at him would wake him. He reached the bathroom door and glanced over at the chair. Something was on it, but he couldn't tell what it was.

He crouched next to the chair and stared down, trying to figure out what the dark shape was. If he hadn't known better, he would have thought it was a snake coiled on the chair. Finally he realized it was a military-style pistol belt and a canteen. Now he stood and moved around the chair until he came to the curtained window.

Opposite him, near the bed, Fetterman was on his hands and knees, checking the floor slowly. There was nothing for him to find, other than the boots, shoes and briefcase.

Gerber reached the wardrobe. He touched its side, running his fingers lightly over it. He worked his way around the front and then down the center until he touched the knobs. There was no sign of a lock.

Gerber knew the revolver had to be in the wardrobe. It was the only place the gun could be, other than under the general's pillow, and Gerber didn't think that was likely. If the general had a hidden weapon, it would be the Colt Commander 9 mm automatic issued to all generals. It wouldn't be the bulky six-shooter. One was for show, the other for protection.

He touched the knob, grasped it and pulled on it. Nothing. He released the pressure, took a deep breath and tried again. There was a sharp, quiet click, and the door sprang open. Gerber froze, but the general didn't stir. His breathing remained the same.

The interior of the wardrobe was black. Gerber reached in, felt the rough cloth of jungle fatigues, then shirts and pants. He knelt and ran his hands over the items on the shelf at the bottom. A shaving kit, a bottle of something, shoes and a knife in a sheath.

And then he found it. His fingers touched the grip of the revolver and then found the tooled leather of the gun belt. He leaned in slightly and slowly lifted the gun belt. When it was free of the shelf, he pulled it toward him, rocking back on his heels. Then he stood up and moved away from the wardrobe without closing the door.

Fetterman had stood up and was looking down at the general. Gerber moved around the foot of the bed, and Fetterman glanced over at him. Gerber nodded toward the door, the gun belt held out in front of him, proof of their success.

They reached the door. Fetterman opened it and Gerber slid through. An instant later Fetterman was out and shutting the door carefully. Gerber handed the gun belt to Fetterman, then used the key to lock the door again. Then, without worrying about the lights, they headed toward the elevator.

"Stairs," said Fetterman. "There has to be stairs around here."

"Good idea."

They turned down the hallway and found a door that opened into the stairwell. Running down two flights, they opened the door and, when the hall was empty, stepped into it.

"Someone's going to recognize that weapon," said Gerber.

Fetterman took the revolver out of the holster and lifted his fatigue jacket so that he could slip it into the waistband of his pants. Gerber took the gun belt and fastened it around his waist, under his jungle fatigue jacket. "Back to the SOG building?" he asked, grinning.

"Sounds good to me," Fetterman replied.

13

THE CARASEL HOTEL

Gerber faced Morrow over the breakfast table. She looked as if she had gotten up only a few minutes earlier. She didn't appear to be fully awake and she didn't look as if she was interested in eating breakfast.

Gerber, on the other hand, was ready to eat. That was the thing about being in Saigon. There was plenty of food available. It wasn't like being in the field, where men had to live off C-rations and food flown in by chopper or what they could catch and kill. Here there were mountains of food. Everything he could want—fresh fruit, eggs, steak, cereal, real milk, juice and coffee. Anything and everything. So, while Morrow sipped coffee and looked as if she were about to fall asleep again, Gerber had a big breakfast of fried eggs, steak, hash browns and as much orange juice as he could drink.

Once the waitress, a Vietnamese woman who looked as if she'd been up all night, had taken the order and disappeared, Gerber said, "I need a favor."

"Too late," said Morrow.

"What do you mean, too late?"

She looked up at him, then rubbed a hand over her face. "I think that sometime in the next ten or fifteen minutes I'm going to pass away. Just fade away, never to be heard from again. Sometime very soon."

"Before you go," said Gerber, "could you do me one little favor?"

"I'll try."

"We need an article...something that'll get some play here in Saigon about Sergeant Fetterman. About his skill with a revolver. Something about him being a new Wyatt Earp, quicker than a snake."

"Good God, why? I thought you Special Forces people were trying to play down that image. You're into civic action and helping the Vietnamese help themselves." She stopped, sipped her coffee, then said, "Oh, never mind. I understand."

The waitress appeared, carrying several dishes containing Gerber's eggs, steak and potatoes. When she was gone again, Gerber said, "We need as much local publicity as we can get."

"Why Fetterman?"

Gerber looked at her. "Because I lost a coin toss."

"Mack, between you and me, is this a good idea? Aren't you kind of walking into an ambush?"

Gerber sprinkled his food with pepper and sat back. He picked up the glass of juice, drank from it, then set it down. "Not really. We've got a Vietnamese running around shooting Americans—"

"Which is part of war."

"Granted. Killing the enemy is part of war. But there are rules, and he's no longer playing by them. We've been given the job of eliminating the guy." He knew he was speaking out of turn, but he needed her help.

"What I really want to know is why is it always you? Always you and Tony, stuck with the dirty jobs."

Gerber ignored the breakfast, which was growing cold. "The reason is simple," he said. "And if I tell you, it's going to sound as if I'm bragging."

"It's because you're good," she said tiredly. "You're so damn good at it."

"The reward for doing your job well is to get stuck with all the dirty jobs. I talked to a man who commands a leg outfit. Those men who are good in the field are in demand. Those who fuck it up are sent to the rear and given what some consider the worst assignments— bunker duty at night, for example—but which are really a breeze."

"Doesn't sound that easy," said Morrow.

"Except you're on the line at night, and because you pulled the duty, you're excused from all the really shit details during the day. You can sleep in, eat when you get up, all because you sat up all night in a bunker where the enemy hasn't even dropped a mortar round in eight weeks. The men who should get that assignment are in the field risking their lives daily because they're good at what they do. The rewards for being good are the truly dangerous assignments."

Morrow drained her coffee, then reached over to grab his orange juice. "Just what do you want said in this article of yours?"

"That Tony is a top gun. He can't be outdrawn in the competitions held by the Special Forces." Gerber grinned. "Make sure you mention, stress, that it's the Special Forces. That should make Billy salivate."

"Billy?"

"Never mind," said Gerber. "We need an article that'll make him have to face Fetterman. Then he'll come to us, and that'll mean we won't have to search for him."

"I can probably get something in the English language afternoon papers."

"And talk it up," said Gerber. "Tell everyone about it. That way the VC will have to overhear it."

"Of course."

Gerber picked up his knife and fork and looked at his breakfast. Before he could take a bite, Fetterman appeared at the side of the table. "I think you'd better come with me," the master sergeant said.

Morrow looked up at him. "What's this, Tony? No 'Good Morning'?"

"We don't have a problem with the special equipment, do we?" Gerber asked.

"Oh, no, sir. This is something else." He turned toward Morrow. "Good morning, Robin."

"Congratulations on your new skill. I hear you're the fastest gun in the East."

"I like to think so. Captain?"

"I just got my breakfast."

"Yes, sir, I can see that."

"Is this something that can't wait until I've finished eating?"

"Of course it could," said Fetterman, "but it's very important. We should return to Tan Son Nhut."

"You're enjoying this, aren't you?"

"Yes, sir. You're the one who thought you could slide away and grab a good breakfast while I had to sit around with Kepler and the boys at Tan Son Nhut, toiling in the early-morning hours with no help from anyone."

"What's going on?" asked Morrow.

"We've got a couple of things we need to discuss," said Fetterman.

"You're not hitting the field, are you?"

"Nope," Fetterman said. Then he looked at Gerber. "Captain?"

Gerber stood, pulled a wad of MPCs from his pocket and dropped the money on the table. "You don't mind this, do you, Robin?"

"Oh, no. I love being abandoned after being dragged out of a sound sleep."

Gerber looked at the breakfast one last time. He picked up a piece of toast, then said, "Lead on."

Fetterman and Gerber left the restaurant, walked to the elevator and took it down. They crossed the cavernous lobby, which was nearly deserted at that time of the morning. The sun was just coming up. Fetterman opened the door before the Vietnamese doorman could get there.

"I've got a jeep," said Fetterman.

"Don't you always?"

They moved to the sidewalk and then along it. There were still people out and about, no doubt the last of the night crowd and the beginnings of the morning crowd. The two groups mingled carefully, as if frightened of each other.

They reached the jeep and Fetterman started to climb behind the wheel. Gerber stood still for a moment, then said, "I think I'd like to drive."

Fetterman shrugged. "Go right ahead."

Gerber moved around and got in behind the wheel. He held out his hand, and Fetterman gave him the key for the padlock. He used it to free the wheel, dropped the chain onto the floor, started the engine, then turned and watched the traffic. When he saw an opening, he pulled out quickly.

They hurried through the city and came to the gate at Tan Son Nhut. There were thousands of Vietnamese standing in line, waiting for a chance to enter. It was a long line, and there were a half-dozen men in fatigues using flashlights to examine ID cards as they waved people on to the base.

Gerber worked his way through the crowd and joined the short line of vehicles. The guard there looked at Gerber, saw the captain's bars sewn to the collar of his jungle fatigues and saluted.

Once through, they drove over to the SOG building. Gerber parked, reached down and picked up the chain, looping it up through the wheel. Both men got out and walked toward the front door of the building.

"Now," said Gerber, "what's so important that I couldn't finish my breakfast?"

Fetterman opened the door and let Gerber walk through. When the door was closed, he said, "Billy's been at it again."

"What have you got?"

"Kepler came in a little while ago and said that the body of a man who's been missing for a couple of days turned up on the road leading to their camp. There was a number stuck in one of his pockets."

"Shit," said Gerber. "I guess that if we didn't believe it before now, we sure have to after this."

"Yes, sir."

"Robin's putting the stuff in the paper for us. I guess we need to get to the range for some practice." He stopped, then asked, "Kepler have any clue as to where Billy might be hiding his camp?"

"Says he can narrow it down to a specific part of Three Corps. It's up in that area where we were before."

"Let's go talk to him and see what he has to say."

MORROW SAT QUIETLY for a moment, then suddenly felt hungry. She reached across the table and picked up the plate. Setting it in front of her, she picked up a fork and took a bite. It was warm, not hot, but then it was free. That made it taste even better.

She ate the meal slowly, thinking about what Gerber had said. It was obvious he was trying to get information into the hands of the VC. That was the only reason to put something in the local press. That and to talk to everyone who would listen. Get the VC involved, and the word might get back to the man they wanted to climinate.

She sat back and wondered about the nature of war and then about the nature of this war. It certainly wasn't being conducted in the way she thought wars should be fought. Gerber was trying to find an enemy soldier, a specific soldier, so he was going to advertise in the paper. Well, it wasn't really an advertisement, but it amounted to almost the same thing.

Morrow finished the breakfast Gerber had ordered, then stood up and walked out of the restaurant. She used the stairs to walk up to her room, where she took a quick shower, brushed her teeth and combed her hair again. Then she dressed and hurried to the office, but when she got there she wasn't sure what she was going to do. She sat at her desk and rolled a sheet of paper into her typewriter. Then, as the rest of the staff came in, she began to type, making up the story as she went along.

Ignoring her colleagues, Morrow wrote about Master Sergeant Anthony B. Fetterman, the fastest draw in the American Army. He was in the same league as Billy the Kid and Wild Bill Hickok. No one could beat him. She laid it on thick, wondering how much was true and how much was hype.

When she finished the story, she pulled it out of the typewriter, read it over and shrugged, not knowing whether it would do the job or not. Then, glancing to the right, she saw that her boss, Mark Hodges, was in his glass-enclosed office.

She walked over, leaned in and waited as he made a production of lighting his cigar. When it was going, the tip glowing orange and a cloud of blue smoke around his head, she asked, "Mind if I go over to the *Stars and Stripes* office?"

"There something going on there?" he asked.

"Not really. I've got a story I want to check out with them."

Hodges puffed on his cigar for a moment, glanced up at the ceiling as if there were something interesting written there, then said, "As long as you're not giving them anything without getting something in return."

"Not at all."

"Then go. But get back by noon."

"Sure." She turned and walked out of the city room, feeling as if she were betraying Fetterman in some way.

LOOKING AT THE MAP, Gerber said, "Maybe we'd better head out there and take a look around." He pointed at Fetterman. "You could wear that fancy revolver. Might get word to Billy faster than anything else we do."

"We'll be going into an ARVN compound," Fetterman reminded him. "Remember what happened the last time we ran into the ARVN while we were there."

"But there are fifty Americans in the camp, too," said Gerber. "There shouldn't be a problem."

Kepler moved forward and sat down at the table. He glanced from one man to the other. "My sources don't have Billy the Zip in the area, but that doesn't mean anything. I think if we show up with the right attitude, word will get back to Billy quickly. He'll come out in search of us. We could blunder into each other.''

"And if we're there," said Gerber, "and something comes up, we can get to Billy faster."

"Then let's go," said Fetterman.

"Derek," said Gerber, "make arrangements to get us transport out there and then get on the horn to Captain Bromhead at Song Be. I want a strike company standing by in case we need help."

"How much should I tell him?"

"Just get the company standing by. We might not need anything, but I want to know we can get a hundred guys in to help us if we need it."

"Yes, sir."

Gerber looked at his watch, then to Fetterman. "I figure we've got thirty minutes on the range. Certainly no more than thirty minutes."

"I won't need it," said Fetterman.

"Tony, I'm going to take a page from Sergeant Tyme's book. He'd insist that you fire the weapon just so that you understand it. With a handgun, especially one like that, you'll need to put a few rounds through it. Learn a little about it before you need it."

"Of course," said Fetterman. "I wasn't thinking."

"We'll hit the range in the back. Derek, alert me the minute you have things arranged."

"Yes, sir."

Fetterman stood up. The gun belt was buckled around his waist. He pulled the revolver out, held it up, then spun the cylinder as if he were a cowboy in an old movie. "I'll say one thing about this gun. It's got a beautiful balance."

"Let's get moving," said Gerber. He walked to the door and waited for Fetterman. The two of them moved to the rear of the SOG building and passed through the supply area, where there was equipment, weapons, uniforms and rations from a dozen different countries. The place looked like a giant international surplus store. They passed the showers, latrine and a few cots set up for the men who were about to go into isolation or those coming off a mission and who needed a fairly secure area. Eventually they came to a cinder-block wall that had a steel door in the middle of it. On the other side was a range set up for zeroing weapons and practice. Targets could be set at twenty-five meters, fifty meters, one hundred, two hundred and three hundred. The shooter had a choice of bull's-eyes or man-size silhouettes.

"What do you want?" asked Gerber. "Twenty-five?"

"I doubt I'll be shooting at any greater range, given the circumstances."

Gerber moved in front of the firing positions, which were all vacant. It was an open area with a short wall behind which those firing stood. He found a stack of targets, grabbed one and set it up. That finished, he retreated to the firing line.

Fetterman faced the cardboard man, the revolver now tied down low. He touched the butt of the six-gun, adjusted the holster, then nodded at Gerber. "I'm ready."

"On the count of three."

"Go."

Gerber hesitated, then said, "One, two, three."

On three Fetterman drew and fired one round. He moved with snakelike quickness, the motion of his hand blurred by the speed. As he pulled the revolver, he thumbed back the hammer and, when the barrel was lined up on the silhouette, he fired. One shot.

"Again?" asked Gerber.

"That's all I need."

"Okay," said Gerber, laughing. He stepped over the wall and walked to the target. There was a single hole in it, right between where the eyes would be. He glanced at Fetterman and shrugged.

"It's a good weapon, Captain. I knew it was when you handed it to me. Fine craftsmanship. A precision tool."

"I thought the current thinking was to fire at the chest, the biggest target."

"I could do that if you think I should," he replied, but he didn't mean it.

Gerber came back and suggested, "Why don't you fan off a quick six? See what you can do with that."

Fetterman nodded. He opened the revolver, spun the cylinder and extracted the spent shell. Replacing it, he pulled the hammer to the half-cocked position and spun the cylinder again to make sure everything was set. "I'm ready."

Again Gerber counted and again Fetterman drew. This time it seemed as if there was a single, drawn-out detonation. Not a series of them, but just one. Fetterman finished shooting, blew the smoke from the barrel, then twirled the six-gun and slipped it into the holster.

"Impressive," Gerber marveled. "Very impressive."

"It's all in the wrist," said Fetterman.

Gerber walked up to the target, expecting to see six bullet holes in the chest, near where the heart would be. That wasn't the case. All six were in the forehead, again between the eyes, and all of them could be covered with a half-dollar.

"Grouped the shots," said Fetterman.

"Tony, there isn't a word that I'm going to say about this from now on. You do it your way."

"I always do."

"You going to need any more practice?"

"No, sir. I think I've got it down now." He wiped his hand on the front of his jungle fatigues. "This is one beautiful weapon."

"We'll have to make sure we get it back to the general when we're done," said Gerber. He took down the target and studied the six bullet holes in the head.

"I could have made the group much smaller," said Fetterman, "but then it would be hard to tell if all six were hits or if I'd missed."

"I think I'd believe you regardless." There was a banging on the metal door. "Come on in!" yelled Gerber.

Kepler opened the door and leaned in. "We're all set. Chopper's on the way in, and Captain Bromhead said there was no problem with the troops as long as we arrange transport to get them off Song Be."

"I assume you did," said Gerber.

"Laid on if we should need it."

"Tony, are you ready?"

Fetterman reloaded the revolver. "I'm as ready as I'll ever be."

"Then let's go see if we can find Billy the Zip."

14

MACV-SOG, TAN SON NHUT

The chopper was sitting on the tarmac outside the building, the turbine whining quietly and the blades slashing through the air with an almost inaudible swish. Kepler, along with Marsh and Laptham, already sat in the back. The door gunner, wearing a chicken plate, flight helmet and gloves, stood next to his M-60, leaning against it.

Gerber ducked slightly and ran forward under the blades of the chopper. As he climbed up into the cargo compartment, Fetterman followed him. When the master sergeant was on board, the door gunner got into the well behind his weapon. The chopper sat there for a moment as the roar of the turbine increased and the blades began to pop loudly. Then they lifted off, hovered and turned, climbing out across the runways.

Gerber settled back but didn't watch the landscape under him. He didn't want to see the deep greens or the small villages or the stretches of rice paddies. Instead, he stared straight ahead at the bouncing needles on the instrument panel. He studied them as if they were the most interesting things he had ever seen. Gerber was trying hard not to worry about the mission.

After thirty or forty minutes, the noise of the aircraft changed and they began a shallow descent. Gerber turned so that he could look out the cargo compartment door. Below was the circular shape of a fire support base's perimeter. There was a large bunker in the center, the top covered with radio antennae.

They circled the base once, and as they passed over the road where the body had been found, Gerber spotted trails in the tall grass. There were a dozen different trails that seemed to converge in a shallow ditch. The grass in the ditch was bright green where the men moving around in it had disturbed the red dust. The main trail led to the road, then turned and snaked back into the jungle.

Fetterman had shifted around so that he could look down at the open field on the northern side of the camp. He glanced back at the jungle, then returned his attention to the camp.

They approached it, coming down slowly, moving toward a rising cloud of purple smoke. The pilots put the nose of the aircraft into the purple, then slowly leveled out until the skids settled onto the ground.

Gerber slipped across the troop seat and jumped out. He could smell the burning gunpowder of the smoke grenade as he ducked down and hurried away from the chopper. As soon as the others joined him, the helicopter took off, climbing back up into a nearly cloudless blue sky.

When the helicopter was gone and silence had settled back onto the camp, an American officer appeared. He walked up to Gerber and said, "Good morning, Captain. I'm Captain McCarthy. How can I help you?"

"Let's get off the helipad," said Gerber.

They all walked back between a couple of bunkers where men had set up lawn chairs and were now attempting to improve their tans. A clothesline was strung between two of the bunkers. Socks and OD T-shirts flapped in the slight breeze. Sitting near one of the clothesline poles was a man reading a paperback novel. He didn't look up as the small party walked by.

"Your men can grab a cup of coffee in the mess hall if they want," said McCarthy.

"Tony, you come with me," said Gerber. "The rest of you stick together."

"Mess hall's over there," said McCarthy, pointing at a low wooden building made mostly of screen and plywood.

As Kepler and the others disappeared, heading toward the mess hall, McCarthy took Gerber and Fetterman down into the commo bunker. Once they were inside, away from the Vietnamese who might be listening, McCarthy asked again, "What can I do for you?"

"You found a body this morning?" probed Gerber.

"American. Been dead about a day. A couple of bullet holes in him, but no sign that anything else had been done to him. No sign of torture."

"And a number?" asked Fetterman.

McCarthy looked at Fetterman, then told Gerber, "A single sheet of folded paper stuck into his pocket."

"Any ID on the man?"

"Nope. Just the sheet of paper. I've put in a call to graves registration, but they haven't been out to collect the body yet."

"Can we see it?" asked Fetterman.

McCarthy looked at him again. "There any good reason for that?"

"Might be," said Gerber.

"What's going on here?" asked McCarthy. "We normally don't get a chopper full of Green Berets out here to look at the body of a dead man."

Gerber shrugged, unsure of what to say. He didn't know how much was supposed to be classified and how much was common knowledge. Besides he'd already said quite a bit to Morrow. Finally he said, "We're chasing a North Vietnamese officer, and this is something he might have been involved in."

"Shit, sounds like a murder."

"Something like that," said Gerber.

McCarthy stared at Gerber for a moment, then nodded. "Well, come along."

They left the commo bunker and walked across the compound toward a tent. The flaps were up. Inside, they could see a single body zipped into a body bag. As they approached they could hear flies buzzing around it, trying to get inside the bag.

They entered the tent, and Fetterman knelt near the body. He worked the zipper down and stared at the dead man. He spotted the two bullet holes in the fatigue jacket, saw the blood-encrusted uniform and realized the man had been shot once in the back. Standing, he said, "I'm ready, Captain."

McCarthy zipped up the body bag. "Satisfied?"

"Thank you," said Fetterman.

"Now what?" asked McCarthy.

"Have you got any patrols out?" asked Gerber.

"Nothing today. Everything's been pulled in for a stand-down. Why?"

"I noticed trails in the grass out toward the road as we flew in. I assume you found the body along the road out there."

"Yes."

"Then it would seem to me that a patrol following those trails back might lead to the enemy."

McCarthy remained silent.

"We could scout it out," said Fetterman.

Gerber turned to McCarthy. "We'll need to get some equipment from you. Rations, water, and I'd like a force to stand by in case we need some help."

McCarthy glanced at the body bag, wiped the sweat from his face and took a deep breath. "I can't promise much."

"What in hell's the problem?" asked Gerber sharply.

"I've got two companies of Vietnamese," snapped McCarthy, "and only fifty Americans. Both Vietnamese companies are riddled with VC. I can't trust them. Any of them."

Gerber took a deep breath. He glanced to the rear at the center of the camp. Four Vietnamese were walking along, each armed with an M-16 and wearing American-style fatigues. They were being paid with American tax money, and they, any of them, might have no loyalty to the Saigon government at all. At the first sign of trouble they might run or they might turn on the Americans. Gerber understood McCarthy's attitude. It was the attitude of a man who didn't know who his friends were, or whether he would be murdered during the night by a supposedly loyal Vietnamese.

"Captain," said Fetterman, "let's walk around the camp for a moment, then see if we can follow the trail."

Gerber nodded. "Okay."

There wasn't much in the camp that Fetterman wanted to see. What he wanted to do was let the Vietnamese see the fancy revolver he was wearing. If the strike companies were as riddled with VC as McCarthy thought, it would be no time at all before Billy heard about the American with the fancy six-gun.

When they were finished their tour of the camp, they walked over to the mess hall, where Kepler and the other two men sat drinking coffee. There were a dozen tables, each surrounded by four chairs, a counter designed to serve the food, a rack for metal trays, and two huge floor fans, only one of which was roaring. Kepler stood up. "Want a cup, sir?"

"I'd like something colder," said Gerber.

"We've got Kool-Aid," said McCarthy, pointing at a large metal tub.

Gerber walked over, picked up a cup from the stack and looked down into the red liquid in the tub. A single block of ice floated in the Kool-Aid. He filled his cup, drank some and then moved toward the table where Kepler and the others sat. When he finished the Kool-Aid, he set the cup on the table. "If everyone's ready."

"We're right behind you," Kepler said.

Gerber turned to McCarthy. "We'll be at the gate in about ten minutes."

"I'll have everything you want there." He turned and walked toward the screen door.

"Not much help," said Fetterman.

"Can't blame him," said Gerber, "given the circumstances. Hell, we've already had a run-in with the ARVN around here and we were here for only an hour. He's got to live with them."

With that, they all got up and walked toward the door. They crossed the compound and reached the gate. McCarthy had indeed come up with the extra equipment. Gerber and Fetterman distributed it, and when McCarthy appeared again, Gerber said, "We should be back by dusk. If we don't make radio contact or return by then, you'd better start thinking in terms of a search party."

"Thank you," said McCarthy sarcastically. "I don't have anything else to do."

"I knew you'd appreciate it," Gerber said.

One of the Vietnamese opened the gate. Fetterman exited, moved to the side of the road and began to walk along it. Laptham, Marsh and then Kepler followed. Gerber hesitated, then turned to McCarthy. "Thanks for your help."

"It wasn't much."

"Might have been enough." With that, Gerber left the camp and fell in behind Kepler.

VAN AWOKE in the middle of the morning, bathed in sweat. He had dreamed about Williams, the man who had outdrawn him. But this time there had been no rifleman in the jungle to protect him. He'd had to face the enemy by himself, and Williams had shot him to pieces. First his hands and then his elbows and finally his knees. He'd been helpless, unable to fight back, and that had scared him badly.

He sat up quickly, glanced out the window and saw that everything was just as it was supposed to be. His men moved around in the gloom of the jungle. Some of them carried their weapons and some didn't. Some wore a complete uniform and some didn't. There were no prisoners in the camp, so their attitude was slightly different now. There was no one to impress, except for their own officers, and it was too late for that.

He stood up and moved to the window. There wasn't much going on. The men were taking it easy, sitting around as the jungle heated up like a steam bath. Van moved to the rear and picked up a towel. He wiped the sweat from his chest and from under his arms, then ran the towel over his head. Tossing the towel aside, he picked up a fatigue shirt, donned it, then retrieved his gun belt, buckling it around his waist.

He moved to the front of the hut, to the room that served as his headquarters, and sat down behind the desk. He looked at the papers there, then pushed them aside. A depression hung over him, and he didn't know what it was or why. Maybe it was because the gunfights were beginning to bore him. Or maybe it was because they weren't dangerous. He knew the outcome before he entered the circle. There was a tap at the door, and one of his men entered. Van looked at him. "Yes, Comrade?"

"We have some news."

"What?"

"There's an American nearby with a revolver like yours. Our allies at the ARVN camp have seen him."

"A six-gun like mine?"

"Yes, Comrade. In the same kind of holster. He's left their camp and is walking into the jungle."

Van felt the depression vanish suddenly. He glanced at his own side where his revolver and holster hung. Another gunfighter in Vietnam? Someone else who understood what it meant when two men faced each other? "Was there any other information?"

"The man is supposed to return to the camp this evening. They don't know if he's going to stay the night or return to his home base."

"Do they know where he came from?"

"No, Comrade, only that he arrived in a helicopter and that he's left the camp on foot."

"I want a patrol ready to leave the camp in fifteen minutes."

"Yes, Comrade."

IT WAS VERY EASY to follow the trail to the jungle. There were wide paths pushed through the grass. It was as easy as driving down a four-lane highway. But the trail seemed to vanish the instant they reached the jungle. Fetterman entered the trees, crouched for a moment, then found a faint indication that the enemy had been there the night before.

Gerber moved closer. "You find it?"

"Easy. They came from that direction. Scuff marks here, and the vegetation's been stepped on here. See that rough place on the bark that's slightly discolored? Someone bumped it in the night."

"Can you follow it all the way back to their camp?"

"I think, sir, that they came straight from their camp. If I line up these clues here, they're going to point us in the right direction. That's even if I don't find another sign."

Gerber shook his head. "Shit. We go to all this trouble, steal a general's fancy revolver, and now you tell me we didn't need to do it."

"We haven't found him yet," said Fetterman.

"True enough."

With that, Fetterman moved deeper into the jungle. He moved slowly, his eyes on the ground, searching for signs that the enemy had been there. He glanced upward, just in case, and then back at the jungle floor. The men strung out behind him.

Fetterman followed the trail slowly, lost it once, then found it again. They moved through the wide valley, along the stream and came to the point where it narrowed. Fearing an ambush, Fetterman stopped. When everyone was in place, he sneaked up the slope and came down behind the entrance to the narrow valley. There was no one hiding there. He could tell the VC had been there, but not recently. Bunkers had been built, but they hadn't been used in several months. They were overgrown with vegetation, and the top of one had collapsed. If Charlie returned, he could have rebuilt it in a couple of hours if he wanted to.

They passed through that area and found the trail again, where it crossed the stream, following it up the slope and along it, just below the crest. Fetterman halted them every ten or fifteen minutes, giving them a chance to rest, but more importantly, giving them a chance to listen to the sounds of the jungle around them.

They all moved silently, trying to leave no sign for the VC. They didn't talk, didn't smoke and didn't cough or sneeze. They set their feet down carefully, feeling with their toes for trip wires and pressure plates, even though the VC didn't usually booby-trap their own backyard.

They kept at it, moving deeper into the triple-canopy jungle, until the sun was just a memory. They could smell the humidity in the air. Each man sweated heavily, turning his jungle fatigues black.

After two hours Fetterman held up his hand. The men spread out in a loose circle. No one moved or said anything. They stayed where they were. Fetterman eased his way to the rear, where Gerber was crouched near the base of a giant teak tree that looked as if it were holding up the canopy.

"Got some movement. Coming toward us," the master sergeant said.

"You seen them?"

"Not yet. Heard them. They're very good, but they still made enough noise for me to hear them."

"Then we'll wait and see who they are."

Fetterman returned to his position in the security ring. He crouched down, sliding to the right so that the branch of a thorn bush protected him somewhat.

The enemy came up out of the jungle. They were a ragtag bunch dressed in black pajamas, fatigues or a combination of the two. They all carried AK-47s, though. And right in the middle of them was a Vietnamese officer wearing a cowboy holster tied down low as if he were looking for a gunfight.

Fetterman waited for them to pass, giving them ten minutes to get away from him. Then he slipped to the rear to where Gerber lay, trying to sink into the jungle floor. The master sergeant leaned close, his voice barely audible. "Billy the Zip just walked by me."

Gerber nodded. "I know. I saw."

"So, what are we going to do about it? Follow and ambush him?"

Gerber shook his head. "We know he takes prisoners. Let's follow his trail back to his camp and see if there are any prisoners there. Once we've cleared the camp, we can take him out."

"I'd rather just ambush him," said Fetterman.

Gerber grinned. "We go to all that trouble to get you a good revolver, and now you don't want to use it."

"I'll use it," said Fetterman. "I just think ambush makes better military sense."

"Sure, if all we wanted to do was kill him. But we need to kill the myth, too. Don't forget that," said Gerber.

"I'm trying," said Fetterman. "I'm trying real hard."

15

IN THE JUNGLES NEAR
THUAN LOI

It took them another hour to reach the enemy camp. Fetterman took them to it directly, skirting the path that had been cut by the VC as they had carried Williams to the American camp. The Americans came to the edge of the jungle and halted there. Fetterman waved them to the side, then moved to the edge, where he could look out over the enemy camp.

There wasn't much to see. A few mud-and-thatch hootches were scattered around a wide-open central area. Cages were suspended from trees. There was a hootch with a stone fireplace at one end and a pit for outdoor cooking, a louvered screen over it to disperse the smoke. And in the center of the camp was a large circle surrounded by a low wall.

There were a few armed men in the camp. One or two were carrying AKs, but the rest looked like soldiers on any base. Their weapons were close, but they weren't holding on to them. Some of the men wore black pajamas. Others were dressed in bright green fatigues. No one looked too interested in what was happening in the jungle around them.

Gerber slipped forward carefully, then knelt next to Fetterman. The master sergeant nodded at the circle. "That look familiar?" He kept his voice low so that no one would overhear.

Although Gerber didn't answer, the circle did look familiar. He'd seen a similar setup in a movie. Clint Eastwood and Lee Van Cleef had shot it out in such a circle in a gunfight where only one of them had survived.

"Looks like the stories are true," said Gerber. "We've got proof now."

"Scope out the situation?" asked Fetterman.

"Quietly and carefully. I want a count of the number of men down there, and I want every building located and identified. Then we'll move in and wait for Billy."

"Yes, sir."

Marsh was left behind with the radio and extra equipment. He'd provide a rear guard if they needed it. Kepler and Laptham would circle to the right, checking out that side of the camp. Gerber and Fetterman would move to the left. They would take no more than an hour. If they met on the other side, fine. If they didn't, they'd retreat to the ARVN base, where they'd decide what to do.

That decided, they moved out, working their way along the edge of the camp, moving silently and slowly. They kept to the shadows, using the dark patches to hide. Occasionally they'd stop to observe the camp, watching the men move around. They identified one barracks, the mess hootch and a building they thought was the headquarters. There was a stockade and, of course, the cages. All of them were empty.

Fetterman tried to get a count of the enemy soldiers in the camp. He put the number at twenty, including a single woman, who he'd noticed walking from the headquarters to the mess hootch. Although she was wearing green fatigues, it was obvious she was a woman because of her long hair. Too many of the men, especially the NVA, liked to cut their hair quite short. It was a status symbol with them, and gave the Americans a way to tell the real farmers from the soldiers masquerading as farmers.

They settled in for a while, studying the camp. Men moved from the barracks to the mess hootch. One man came out of the mess hootch, tossed something into the pit, then stepped back. Flames shot up for a moment, then disappeared as smoke began to boil up and out of the pit. It hit the strange chimney, bounced around among the louvers until it was little more than pale wisps, then drifted up toward the triple canopy.

The VC returned to the mess hootch and didn't come back out. The woman did. But she didn't walk toward the pit. She headed for the headquarters building.

"You see enough?" asked Fetterman.

Gerber nodded. There didn't seem to be a routine. Everyone just stumbled around. No sign of guards around the camp and no sign of any patrols, other than the one they had passed on their way in. He pointed back in the direction they had come.

They found Marsh and joined him. Gerber used the time to drink some water, sharing his canteen with Fetterman and Marsh. Kepler returned with Laptham, and they all held a hurried conversation with Gerber, who told them that if they moved swiftly, they could have the camp secured before Billy and his men had a chance to return.

"Take them all out and then let Billy and his men walk in," Gerber said. "Capture the whole bunch quickly."

"Billy's reputation, Captain," said Fetterman.

"I know what you're thinking, Tony, but if we can take him without firing a shot, he's not going to have a reputation left for us to worry about. We'll take them about dusk, as soon as it's dark enough for us to operate easily. We'll take the whole camp then."

But before anyone could respond, there was a noise behind them, a faint sound of metal against metal. The Americans settled in, hiding in the jungle.

The patrol they had passed was returning to camp. They came down off the slight ridge, walked around a large tree, then fanned out into camp. Billy the Zip walked past everyone and headed straight for his headquarters building. He still wore his holster tied down low. He didn't look right or left.

As he disappeared into the headquarters, Fetterman asked, "We still going to take them?"

"Yeah," said Gerber. "After dark."

"Until then?"

"We lie low and watch the camp. Make sure we've got everything spotted."

"Yes, sir," said Fetterman. "We going to capture him?"

Gerber looked at Fetterman and thought about the American soldier they had seen that morning. He thought about how that man must have felt, facing Billy. No real hope of winning because the VC had controlled everything. He thought about how it would feel to get even and he thought about Maxwell and Morrow telling him that Billy had done it before.

"Let's see how things develop before we decide," said Gerber. "It'll depend on how things break."

VAN WASN'T HAPPY about returning to his camp. Not happy about it at all. But as they had come down off the ridge to the narrow passage where they could move out into the wider valley, it was obvious someone had been there recently. Someone other than his men.

He had held there for a few minutes, trying to figure out what to do next. He'd been intrigued by the reports of an American wearing an Old West holster. But now he knew there were Americans behind him somewhere. The only smart thing to do was to get out, return to his camp and wait for another report of the American with the fancy revolver. And that was what he had done.

He and his men had turned around and worked their way back to the camp, using a path they hadn't followed, afraid the Americans might have set up an ambush. They had looped to the east, then back to the west, crossing their original trail once but not moving along it. All the time they had searched for signs of the Americans, who had to be in the jungle somewhere around them.

Finally, when they had approached the camp, he and his men had hesitated in the jungle for a few minutes, making sure nothing was wrong. But everything had seemed peaceful.

Now they were in the camp. Some of his men had headed for their barracks. Others had made for the mess hall. Van had gone to the headquarters building. Once inside, he unbuckled his gun belt and set it on his desk.

Miss Kitty appeared. "You didn't find them?"

"No. They're around somewhere, but we couldn't find them. Maybe tomorrow." He walked behind the desk, sat down and glanced up at the woman. But now he felt no desire for her. He couldn't believe he had ever felt anything for her.

"There are more rumors," she said. "We've received another report, this one from Saigon."

Van leaned back in his chair, wiped a hand over his face, looked at the sweat, then rubbed it on his shirt. "What have you heard?"

"There's an American soldier in Saigon. The report says he's the fastest man alive. He can outdraw anyone and hit anything."

"They don't know about me," said Van.

Miss Kitty sat on the corner of the desk. "Maybe they do. There's a reference to a Vietnamese who thinks he's fast. The claim is that he's never faced an American who knows what he's doing."

Van stared up at her and felt a mounting rage. The room swam in red. He slammed his hand against the desktop, then doubled his fist. "That's not true!" he yelled. "Not true! I can beat anyone they send against me. Anyone."

"Don't yell at me," she said. "I'm only telling you what's being said."

"It's not true." He stood up, whirled and walked to the window. Leaning on the bamboo that reinforced the sill, he stared out at the circular gunfighting area. "There," he said, thrusting his finger out. "That's where we could find out the truth, if the American was brave enough to face me."

"It won't happen," said Miss Kitty. "There's no way he'll come out here."

Van returned to his desk and pulled his revolver from its holster. He fingered the grip with the notches, then ran his hands over the gun as if it were an art object that had been recovered at great cost.

"You're right," he said. "But I could go to him. I could let him know that the question wouldn't be resolved until we faced each other."

"You'd be killed."

"You don't know that," said Van. He thumbed back the hammer of the revolver.

"I mean, you'd be walking into a trap. Thousands of Americans around. Even if you won, they'd cut you down. There would be no escape."

Van sat down and thought about it. Rumors of an American with a revolver like this. Rumors of an American gunfighter who claimed to be faster than any man alive. A man who saw himself as part of a breed that had lived and died during a short period of American history.

Sitting there in his headquarters building, sweating in the late-afternoon heat, Van knew he had found a kindred spirit. He had learned of someone who understood the thrill of facing another man in a circle. He had found someone who would be a worthy opponent . . . if there was some way to meet him.

"It could be done," he said quietly. "A challenge issued to him alone. We could meet to settle the score quietly. There's no reason for anyone else to know about our meeting."

Tran opened the door and entered. He glanced at Van, then at Miss Kitty. "Patrol will be ready to go out in about twenty minutes."

Van rubbed his eyes with the heels of his hands. He looked up and said, "No. Not tonight. Everyone stays in the camp tonight."

"Why?"

"Tomorrow we're going to try to reach Saigon," said Van. "I want everyone rested."

"The whole unit?"

"No," said Van. "Just a platoon. Half the men will remain here, but our operations will be drastically reduced."

"Why?" asked Tran.

Miss Kitty stood up and turned to face Van. To Tran she said, "He wants to face the American gunfighter. He wants to kill him to prove he's the best around."

"Then I should get my rifle ready."

Van was going to tell him not to bother, but hesitated. No one would ever know if he had an edge. That was the way it had been in the Old West. It was the way it always was. The man who planned things out, the one who guaranteed an edge, for himself, was the man who won. He might not need Tran. The American had probably never faced a living, breathing target. He had probably never faced the chance that he could be killed during a gunfight. But that was no reason for Van not to make sure he held the winning cards.

"I'll want to get an early start," he told Tran. "It'll take us several days to get down there."

Tran nodded. "I can begin to put together a list of the proper people to take."

"Good." Van slipped the revolver back into the holster. Then he turned to the window again. "When this is over, everyone in Vietnam will know who I am."

"Yes, Comrade," said Tran. "And they'll be afraid of you. No more gunfights."

"Not true," said Van. "Then they'll come from all over the world. I'll be like the men in the American West. I'll be the top gun, and it'll be the others who will want to kill me and achieve instant fame."

"That's not a good way to live," said Miss Kitty.

"But it's a quick way to die," Tran commented.

"Not if you're good," said Van, looking from one to the other. "Not if you're good."

16

IN THE JUNGLES NEAR THUAN LOI

As they had done during the afternoon recon, they would break into two teams to sweep through the camp. Kepler and Laptham, and Gerber and Fetterman. Marsh would be left behind with the radio so that he could call in assistance if something went wrong. They would silently take out everyone in the camp except for Billy the Zip. They'd work around him so that in the morning he'd be there all alone. It was a good plan. One with a nice, ironic touch to it.

They watched while the VC and NVA went about their business as the sun set and the dim jungle turned black. The enemy soldiers all trooped to the mess hootch, then headed back to their barracks. There were no military formations, no indications that any guards had been posted and no sign that any patrols had gone out. Even Boy Scouts were better organized.

At midnight Gerber and Fetterman slipped from hiding and worked their way down to the edge of the camp. They stopped there and studied the blackness around them. There were no lights showing, and there was almost no sound. Occasionally they heard someone stumble out to relieve himself in the jungle.

Gerber touched Fetterman on the shoulder, and they moved in slowly, heading for the barracks first. They reached it and crouched at the foot of the wall. If silence hadn't been a consideration, they could have tossed a couple of grenades in and ended any threat there instantly.

Fetterman leaned close, his lips no more than an inch from Gerber's ear. "How you going to do this?"

Before the captain could answer, they heard a noise from inside the building. It sounded as if someone had tripped. There was a mumbled curse in Vietnamese and then the sound of something scraping on the wooden floor. A man appeared in the doorway, then stepped away from the barracks, heading toward the mess hootch.

Without a word Fetterman moved in and killed the man. When the job was done, the master sergeant rolled the body under a hootch, out of the way. He wiped the blade of his knife on the dead man's shirt, then worked his way back to Gerber. "That's one."

"I wonder how Kepler's doing?" Gerber said.

KEPLER AND LAPTHAM MOVED along the edge of the camp, staying in the trees until they were two hundred meters from Gerber and Fetterman. They crouched at the edge of the camp and watched for movement, but the enemy had given up for the night.

Satisfied that there were no sentries, Kepler, moved forward. He bent low, sticking to the blackest of the shadows. When they came to a hootch, they split up.

Kepler inched forward, listening hard. There was someone inside. Maybe one man. Maybe two. He crawled under a window and stood up on the other side, flattening against the thatch on the wall. He glanced in, but the interior was dark. A shadow moved, but it had no distinct shape.

Kepler came around to the front of the hootch. Laptham was kneeling in the shadows. Kepler held up his knife, then nodded at the door. Laptham signaled that he understood. As Laptham came toward him, Kepler entered the hootch slowly, staying low and in the shadows.

He slipped to the right, along the wall, and listened. There was a scrape on the floor that sounded like the tough tire tread of a Ho Chi Minh sandal against rough wood. Staring to the right, Kepler saw movement. A humanlike shape was coming at him.

Afraid he had been spotted, Kepler came up off the floor and stepped toward the shape. He swung his left hand out and grabbed the man behind the head. Jerking him forward, he plunged his knife into the man's chest and felt the blood wash down over his hand and stain his own uniform.

The man groaned deeply. One hand shot out and grasped Kepler's wrist, but it was a weak grip. The enemy soldier sagged, and Kepler grabbed him, holding him upright, then lowered him to the floor.

At that moment he heard a low voice from a darkened corner of the hootch. Kepler froze and listened. Then he turned his head slowly, trying to use his peripheral vision to spot the second man in the hootch.

The enemy soldier was sitting up on the floor, staring straight ahead as he spoke softly. He leaned forward and reached out with a hand as if searching for something on the floor.

Kepler started to move to the right into the shadows, but as he did there was movement to his left. Laptham had slipped in behind him and was staying close to the wall. He struck suddenly, cutting off the stream of soft Vietnamese words. There was a sound of tearing silk, a quiet, desperate moan, then silence.

Kepler turned and moved toward the door. He looked out at the enemy camp. There was no movement or sound from any of the VC or NVA. Just normal jungle sounds—big cats roaring, night birds squawking, insects buzzing.

"Hootch's cleared," whispered Laptham as he leaned close to Kepler.

"Weapons?"

"Shit."

Laptham turned and moved back into the dark, feeling around for the weapons. Kepler heard the quiet click of a bolt being pulled from an AK. There was no way they could carry off all the weapons, but they could take the bolts from them and render them useless except as clubs.

"Ready," said Laptham a moment later.

Kepler glanced to the rear over his shoulder and then moved out of the doorway, molding himself to the frame and keeping his back to the rough thatch. Outside, he slipped to one knee and sucked in fresh air.

He glanced to the right and saw another small hootch. This one had to be the radio shack, with probably a single radio. Kepler held up a hand and pointed at the hootch. Laptham, who had joined him, nodded and stood up. He took a step, froze, then hurried forward, staying in the shadows. There was no sound from him and none from anywhere else in the camp.

GERBER KNEW there would be twenty men in the hootch. At least twenty men. He didn't think they could slip through the whole barracks and kill everyone inside without someone hearing them. Someone would wake up, shout, cough, scream, and that would be it. They'd be stuck in there, outnumbered ten to one.

But then he remembered the stories of VC slipping into a bunker and killing everyone in it except for one man. He'd wake up the next morning and find everyone's throat had been cut sometime during the night. With a few good breaks they could eliminate the threat in the barracks without a sound, just like the ballsy VC.

Gerber slipped back, away from the door, and as he did another Vietnamese soldier came out. The man stopped, looked around, then shrugged. Before he could return to the interior, Gerber struck. He reached up, grabbed the soldier and pulled him back away from the door.

Gerber used his knife, stabbing up under the breastbone. The knife slipped in with only the slightest resistance. It cut through the skin and muscle easily. It pierced the heart, and the man died without a sound. Gerber lowered the corpse to the ground and rolled it over, close to the wall of the hootch.

If they kept coming out, one at a time, it would be damn easy. But they couldn't count on that. They had to go in and try to take them out. Quietly.

Gerber leaned close to Fetterman. "We go in. You take the left. I'll take the right."

"If someone yells?"

"Then we use the M-16s and shoot everyone in sight."

"Yes, sir."

VAN SAT IN THE DARK and thought about the American soldier with the fancy revolver who called himself the fastest man in the world. He thought about the man who was a Special Forces sergeant, one of the super Green Berets who couldn't be defeated. Super soldiers who were the best at their jobs. Van knew that killing such a man would give him the reputation as the most dangerous man alive. People would talk about him for years to come.

He could see the scene in his mind's eye. The hulking American soldier, looking like a giant out of an old fable, towering over him. A huge man with the dreaded green beret plastered to his head. A reckless, arrogant man with a fancy revolver. Van, wearing his fatigues, facing him with his own weapon.

They'd draw at the same time. Van would be faster. Had to be faster. He'd fire once, hitting the American between the eyes. The man's beret would fly off his head, and he would collapse to the ground, blood spurting from his wound. Van would calmly walk over and pick up the six-gun and beret as souvenirs of his victory. Then, while the spectators watched, he would walk away.

Suddenly he opened his eyes, laced his fingers behind his head and stared up at the darkened thatch of the roof. Beside him Miss Kitty rolled toward him. "You awake?" she asked.

"I'm awake," he said.

"What are you thinking about?"

"Killing a Green Beret. Facing down that man in Saigon and killing him."

"You won't be able to set it up the way you have here."

Van tried to see her out of the corner of his eye, but it was too dark. He knew what she was saying. It was something that neither Tran nor she ever mentioned out loud—the fact that Tran sat in the trees with his rifle ready to end a fight if it looked as if Van was going to lose. If he traveled to Saigon, it would be hard to get Tran into position to protect him if he needed it.

"If we're careful," he told her, "we can do it any way we want. It's just a question of setting it all up properly. It's a question of getting an edge."

She reached down, felt his belly and pushed her hand lower under the waistband of his black shorts. She fingered him gently. "Maybe it's time for us to return to the North, now that there are Americans looking for us."

He rolled onto his side so that he was facing her. One hand was under his head. With the other he touched her, first between the breasts and then on the belly. He let his fingers dance over her skin as he reached lower.

"I'm worried about this," she said suddenly. "Very worried."

"Nothing to worry about," said Van, suddenly forgetting about the thrill of killing a Green Beret in a gunfight. His whole attention was focused on her. On her body. "I don't want to talk about it," he said, and leaned forward to kiss her. He could tell she was ready now. There was no reason to wait. She lifted her leg and put her knee on his hip, and as she did, Van pressed himself against her, losing himself in the act.

GERBER WAS CROUCHED at the side of the door, his face held low near the thatch. He could smell it, just like the odor of dried, dirty grass suddenly disturbed by a lawn mower on a hot afternoon. From the interior came the quiet buzz of sleep. A couple of men snored faintly. Across from Gerber, on the other side of the door, was Fetterman. The master sergeant was crouched on the balls of his feet, one hand touching the side of the door and the other holding his knife. He was ready and waiting.

There was no reason to hesitate. Gerber nodded once, and Fetterman slipped into the barracks. As soon as he had cleared the door, Gerber followed, stopping near the corner and looking down the wall. There didn't seem to be any cots in the barracks, just blankets and straw, bamboo mats and a couple of sleeping bags.

One man was sleeping in the corner, his head no more than twelve inches from Gerber's foot. The captain leaned forward and looked down into the man's face. With his left hand he covered the soldier's mouth and nose. As he did that, he struck with the knife, cutting the throat and carotid artery. The blood spurted once, soaking the surrounding thatch.

Gerber moved out of the corner and attacked the next man, who was on his back, facing away from the captain. Gerber liked that. He hit the man in the back with his knee, flattening him on his stomach, then grabbed him by the back of the head and under the chin, jerking the head around. There was a quiet popping of bone and cartilage, and the enemy soldier went limp.

Gerber worked his way down the line of men, using the knife when necessary and snapping the necks when he could. He killed them silently as they slept. When he reached the last soldier, the man sat up suddenly. He stared at Gerber, searching his eyes, then said something quietly in Vietnamese. Gerber nodded, bowed his head slightly and struck. The knife hit bone where there wasn't supposed to be bone and slipped to the right. The man grabbed Gerber's wrist, his fingernails digging in. He started to scream, but Gerber covered his mouth, pressing him back and down.

Now the solder tried to roll free. He kicked out once, but missed Gerber completely. Gerber turned with the kick, used the momentum against the man and rolled him over onto his belly. He dropped a knee in to the middle of the man's back and heard the breath rush out of him. Using his knife again, he felt it slip in this time and heard the faint sound of ripping cloth. The enemy bucked once, more of a spasm, and then was still.

"Fucked it up," said Fetterman.

Gerber turned and looked at the master sergeant, who was no more than two inches from him. "Fucked it up good, but that takes care of them in here."

"Let's get out," said Fetterman.

Gerber stood up slowly. His muscles ached and his back hurt. He knew it was from the strain of having to be so quiet and from moving from one man to the next, killing each without warning. In the World he'd be labeled a mass murderer and convicted immediately. No question about it. Here, if anyone ever learned of the deed, he'd probably get a medal for wiping out an enemy platoon with the help of a single NCO.

He stood up. His hands were wet and sticky, covered with the drying blood of dead men. The sleeves of his fatigue jacket were wet to the elbows. The inside of the barracks smelled like a slaughterhouse late in the afternoon in the middle of July.

Gerber knew there were weapons scattered around the floor—twenty or thirty AKs, probably a few pistols and some rifles stolen from Americans. If it was anything like an American billet, there would also be knives, shotguns and probably more than a few grenades. But there was no time to look for them now.

He moved toward the door and hesitated. A slight breeze blew in. It was hot, full of humidity and the odor of rotting vegetation, but compared to the odors and the air in the barracks, it was as fresh and clean as an arctic blast.

Fetterman joined him, and they looked out at the tiny camp. There were only two buildings left to check—the headquarters where Billy the Zip slept and the mess hootch off to the right. If it was anything like an American camp, there would be someone in the mess hootch, either the cook or someone trying to find a midnight snack.

"Let's check out the mess hootch," said Gerber.

"And then?"

"We'll play it by ear."

KEPLER HAD NO TROUBLE in the radio shack. One man was sleeping on the floor. Kepler moved through the open doorway, crouched in the darkness and stared at the man until he turned over onto his back. Then, as he began to sit up, Kepler thrust his knife into the man's chest and slammed his other hand into the bridge of the guy's nose, shattering the bones and driving them back into the surprised VC's brain, killing him instantly.

Standing, Kepler moved to the radio. It was a single unit, not unlike the PRC-25 carried by most American infantry units. He pulled it across the rough wooden table, jerked the antenna leads from the rear, then pulled the power pack off. Kepler wanted to throw it on the floor and stomp on it, but he didn't want to make any noise. So, instead, he picked it up and carried it to the doorway, where he stopped, crouched and waited until Laptham came out of the shadows.

"Got it," whispered Kepler.

"Let's get out, then."

They slipped out of the radio shack and headed toward the headquarters building. Kepler glanced to the right at the cages hanging in the trees. He wanted to cut them down and destroy them, but now wasn't the time. He could do that in the morning, after they had made sure the camp was clear of enemy soldiers.

They stopped near the headquarters. Kepler put the radio on the ground and pushed it under the building, not caring if he ruined it with mud, water or dirt.

"Now," he said quietly, "we wait for the captain and Fetterman."

BOTH FETTERMAN AND GERBER were just outside the door of the mess hootch. They moved in exactly as they had into the barracks, but this time they were disappointed. There was no one inside. The hootch was empty.

They moved out and Gerber stood up, scanning the camp. If Kepler and Laptham had done their job, there wasn't a structure in the camp that hadn't been searched. Everything, except the headquarters, had been cleared. Billy the Zip slumbered on, unaware that his command was gone and that he, along with the one or two people in the headquarters, was alone.

They moved through the camp toward the headquarters. Now they didn't bother staying in the blackest of the shadows. They moved quietly and carefully, but they knew the enemy had been eliminated.

They found Kepler, and Gerber leaned close to him. "You take care of everyone?"

"Yes, sir. Got the radio, too."

"Okay." Gerber pulled back the camouflage cover on his watch and checked the time. "We've got less than an hour to sunup."

"Just enough time to get ready," said Fetterman.

"Derek, go get Marsh, make a radio check and then come back in."

"Yes, sir."

"Tony, let's head for the circle. Laptham, you come with us."

"Yes, sir."

As Kepler headed off, Gerber, Fetterman and Laptham moved toward the circle. They scouted the whole thing, looking for gimmicks and booby traps, but found nothing. The ground was solid, as was the wall. There was nothing to spring up or out to distract the man who didn't know they were there. Nothing to confound or confuse. Just open ground where two men faced each other.

Satisfied, Gerber moved closer to Fetterman. "I can still take over on this."

"I'm the one who practiced," said Fetterman. "You saw what I can do."

Gerber almost told him that it was different, facing a real man with a gun in his hand, but Fetterman knew that. Probably knew it better than Gerber himself.

Gerber checked the time again. "We'd better get ready." He noticed that it was just a little brighter, making it easier to see. The sounds in the jungle were changing. The silence that had settled in just before dawn was beginning to break up. Monkeys, birds, lizards and insects were waking up and greeting the sun.

Fetterman wiped his hands on his jungle shirt. They were caked with blood, which made them stiff. Gerber pulled out his canteen and poured some water into Fetterman's cupped hands so that he could wash them.

"That's good, Captain."

"If you're ready," said Gerber.

Fetterman strode forward, stepped over the wall and ambled to the top of the circle. He could see the headquarters opposite him now. The ground was brighter. Buildings were beginning to take shape and the shadows were fading.

Fetterman stood there for a moment and then, with his hands on his hips, shouted, "Billy! Billy the Zip! I'm calling you out!"

Gerber laughed. It was a line from the worst western ever written.

When there was no answer, Fetterman yelled again. Then he looked at Gerber and shrugged. "I had to say something."

17

THUAN LOI, RVN

The first shout brought Van up out of his sleep. He wasn't sure he'd heard anything, and then he wondered whether Miss Kitty had said something that had somehow gotten confused with something in his dream. The shout came again, and this time he knew it was coming from outside.

"What?" asked Miss Kitty, her voice blurred by sleep. She rubbed an eye.

Van got up, crawled over her and padded to the window. The sun was up, and light was filtering down, creating the green glow he had come to know so well.

The voice came again. "I'm calling you out."

Van turned and looked at the circle with the low wall and saw a man standing at the far side of it. He was a small American dressed in jungle fatigues and wearing a cowboy holster tied down low.

"What? How?" Miss Kitty sputtered.

Van glanced back at her. "I don't know how. I don't know what's happening."

The door behind him burst open. Tran, holding his sniper rifle and a fatigue shirt, came through. He raised the rifle, clutched in his left hand, and pointed it in the direction of the window. "There's an American soldier out there."

"I know that. Where are our soldiers? How did he get out there?"

Tran set the rifle down, leaning it against the foot of the cot. He donned his shirt, buttoning it rapidly. "What are we going to do?"

Van looked at his sniper, at Miss Kitty and then at the man outside. It was obvious what the intruder wanted. Van had heard the words in a dozen western movies. The young punk riding into town always called out the ag-ing gunfighter.

But the man standing in the growing morning light didn't look like a young punk. He looked more like a battle-hardened veteran. He looked like someone who knew the score. And the fact that his own men hadn't come boiling out of their barracks to kill the intruder told Van something more. The situation was critical.

Van returned to the window, but stood off to the side so that he wouldn't be easy to see. He studied the scene in front of him. One man was in the circle, and a couple of others sat in the bleachers where his own men would normally be. There was no sign of anyone else.

"Yo!" yelled the man. "Billy the Zip! You coming out to face me, or are you too frightened?"

"Do you think you can get out into the jungle without being seen?" asked Van.

"I don't know," said Tran. He picked up his rifle, then glanced at Miss Kitty. "Why go into the jungle? I can line up the shot from here."

Van looked at him and realized that the only reason Tran had ever hidden in the jungle was so that his men wouldn't know they were cheating. Tran could stay right here and pick off the American, if they wanted to do it that way.

"Give her a weapon," said Tran, "and we can get them all right now."

"No," said Van. "I'll go out and face him. Just like he wants. You kill the others as soon as I've taken out the man in the circle. Kill them all."

"It'll be a pleasure," said Tran.

Van turned and looked at Miss Kitty. She was still on the cot, looking up at him. "Where are our men?" she asked.

"We'll find that out in a few minutes," said Van. He looked at his fatigues, then shook his head. Instead, he dressed in his gunfighting clothes—a dark green shirt with pearl snaps and white fringe, blue jeans and boots. He buckled on his gun belt and pulled out his revolver, looking at it lovingly. Working the hammer, he spun the cylinder and holstered the weapon.

"I'm ready."

"How do you want to do this?"

"I'll face him as always, but if it looks bad, if he's as fast as the Americans claim, you'll have to shoot him. Then I'll shoot at the men watching." He turned to Miss Kitty. "You'll have to shoot at them, too. Kill them all."

"Of course," she said, grinning.

Van moved to the door. He glanced back at the window. It was much brighter now. The sun was up. Tran was near the window, and Miss Kitty had gotten off the cot. She didn't bother to dress. She picked up an AK and worked the bolt to make sure a round was chambered.

"I'll go meet him now," said Van. Then, just before he stepped out onto the small porch, he added, "These Americans are so stupid."

FETTERMAN WAS ABOUT to shout again, but then he saw a figure emerge. The master sergeant turned to face him. "Come on, Billy. Let's get this thing decided."

Van walked down the three steps and out onto the hard-packed dirt of the compound. He moved slowly, deliberately, his hips swaying. The only thing missing was the jingle of his spurs.

Van stepped over the wall and into the circle. He stopped short, touched the butt of his revolver, then took off his Stetson, wiping at the sweatband. "How you want to do this?"

Fetterman laughed. "The easiest way possible. You and me. One of my men counts to three and we draw."

"And when this is over," said Van, "if I win, then your men kill me?"

"That won't happen, Billy. You'll be dead."

"If I win?"

"Then you go free. Off into the jungle. You'll have an hour's head start. Then, if my boys can find you, they'll cut you down."

"Fair enough," said Van. He glanced to the right, where the barracks stood. "Where are my men?"

"Dead," said Fetterman. "I wanted to make this a fair fight. I didn't want any of your men interfering before we had the chance to learn who's the fastest. It's just you and me. No one else."

"I'm ready," said Van.

Fetterman turned to his men. "Derek, do you want to count this off?"

"Happy to."

Fetterman turned and faced Billy the Zip. He reached down and unhooked the leather loop over the hammer of the stolen revolver. Then he nodded that he was ready.

Van pushed his hat back slightly and licked his lips. He splayed his fingers, flexing them, and then he, too, nodded.

"One," said Kepler, grinning broadly.

As soon as Fetterman shouted the second time, Gerber took off at a run. He leaped the low wall and sprinted between two of the hootches so that anyone in the headquarters wouldn't be able to see him.

He worked his way to the headquarters hootch and crawled up behind it. Listening to the quiet voices inside, he couldn't understand what they were saying, but knew it was something dangerous to Fetterman's health.

He could hear the master sergeant still shouting, drawing attention to himself. Gerber moved to the door in the rear of the headquarters. From the sounds inside, it sounded as if the Vietnamese were on the other side of the hootch, facing away from the door. He didn't know whether there was more than one room, or how the interior was set up, but hoped he could get in without the Vietnamese noticing his presence. He hoped there wasn't a platoon of heavily armed NVA waiting inside. He wanted the game to be played out fairly because he wanted Billy the Zip to know what real fear was.

Fetterman yelled again, and Gerber stepped up onto the notched log that served as steps. Glancing into the hootch, he saw an empty room and entered it slowly, careful not to make any sound. From the other side of the flimsy wall, he could still hear voices. It sounded like two men and a woman, exactly what they had determined the night before.

Gerber moved across the floor and stopped near the door, listening. When he heard one of the men step out onto the porch and then move off toward the circle,

Gerber opened the door. He leaned against it and pushed. As he did, he pointed his rifle through it, hoping he wouldn't have to use it.

Unfortunately the door squeaked as it opened. The man kneeling near the window had his rifle up. As the door opened, announcing Gerber, the man whirled. There was no choice. Gerber fired just once. The round hit the man in the face, blowing off the back of his skull. He fell as if he had been poleaxed.

The woman next to him grabbed at the AK but moved too slowly. Gerber aimed at her belly and she froze. Then, realizing she was nearly naked, she raised a hand to cover her breasts.

Gerber moved into the room and nodded at the door. The woman stood up and walked toward it. Keeping an eye on her, he moved to the dead man and grabbed him by the collar. He dragged the body toward the door, then rolled it across the porch so that it fell to the ground. It landed like a sack of wet cement dropped from four or five feet.

VAN FLINCHED at the sound of the shot. Tran had jumped the gun, but then Van realized something was wrong. The man facing him wasn't falling. None of the Americans were falling. It wasn't right. Then he was aware of a noise behind him. Someone *was* falling. He stared at Fetterman, wondering what had happened.

"Derek," said a voice from behind him, "let's hold off on the counting for a moment. No one draw."

Fetterman lifted his hands slightly, holding them away from his revolver. As that happened, Van turned and stared at the body lying facedown in the dirt. There was a ragged hole in the back of his head. Gray-green brain showed through. Kneeling near the body was Miss Kitty.

In that one minute, Van realized what had happened. The Americans had trumped his ace. They had killed the rifleman and left him there, as naked as the woman, facing an American soldier.

"Shall we continue?" asked Fetterman. "Now that we know it's a fair fight."

Van looked at the man, at the Americans in the bleachers and then back at the one near the body of Tran. Slowly he raised his hands and grinned. "I'm your prisoner."

"Nope," said Fetterman.

"Your Geneva Convention is very clear on the matter. I'm your prisoner. You must treat me according to the rules."

"Nope," said Fetterman. "My government isn't here. Your government isn't here. It's just you and me and that's it. You can draw on the count of three or not. It's your choice. But on the count of three I'm going to draw."

Van shook his head and then held up his hands. "No. That would be murder. You can't do that."

"You're getting more of a chance than your men had last night. Fight or die. I don't care which."

Van pulled his Stetson from his head and threw it away. Then he folded his hands and pleaded, "Please."

"Derek, if you'll be good enough to count again."

"One," said Kepler.

"No!" wailed Van. "You can't do this. It's not fair. It's against your law."

"Two," said Kepler.

Again Van wailed, but this time his hand moved. It dropped to his side, grabbing for the butt of his weapon.

Fetterman saw the motion and drew quickly. As the revolver came out of the holster, he thumbed back the hammer. Without aiming he pointed the barrel and fired. The gun jumped slightly, and the bullet struck with a wet smack. Van was thrown backward by the impact. It looked as if he were going to sit on the wall, and then he tumbled over it, dead before he hit the ground. He never cleared leather.

"Three," said Kepler unnecessarily.

Fetterman walked forward slowly, his six-gun pointing at Billy the Zip. He glanced down at the dead man. There was a single bullet hole in his head, just below the right eye.

Gerber walked forward, pushing the woman in front of him. "Pulled that one a little bit."

"I didn't think the fucker would draw. I thought he'd fall to his knees and beg for his life."

"What would you have done then?" asked Gerber.

"You really want to know, Captain?"

Gerber shook his head. "I already know." He glanced at the three men sitting in the bleachers. "Laptham, get on the horn and see if you can whistle up a chopper."

"Can't land here, sir."

"I know," said Gerber, "but there's an LZ about three klicks south of here. Up along that ridge line. A single ship should be able to extract us."

"Yes, sir."

Fetterman pointed at the woman. "What are you going to do with her?"

"Find her some clothes. We'll take her with us. She's a POW now."

Fetterman turned his attention back to the dead man. He looked small now. Little and mean, a cheat and a coward. Fetterman had known all along that Billy the

Zip wouldn't face anyone alone. He'd known there would be a rifleman somewhere, just in case. But like all cheats, Billy hadn't believed someone else, given a fair shake, might figure it all out. He'd assumed he'd be able to take out anyone with his hidden rifleman.

"Doesn't look like much now," said Gerber.

"No, sir. Looks like the little prick he was." Fetterman took a deep breath. "Maxwell will be happy. The reign of terror's over, and morale can return to its normal low state."

"You're sounding a little down, Master Sergeant."

Fetterman shrugged. "A lot of effort for nothing. Hell, artillery could have done this." He knelt down and pried the revolver out of Billy's fingers. It looked like the twin of the one they'd stolen from the general. He stood up. "You going to tell Robin about this?"

"I don't know what we'll tell her. The story's over here, but there's no way she can print it. We'd both go to LBJ if she did."

"Then the story's dead here, too."

"Deader than hell," said Gerber.

"Yeah," said Fetterman. "I was afraid of that."

18

DONG XOAI, RVN

Sitting on the porch of the same roadhouse where they had had the run-in with the ARVN, Gerber and Fetterman were finally relaxed. The old woman who had been there on the first visit was there again and she was assisted by the young girl who had waited on them the first time. It was as if time hadn't passed at all.

They'd told Maxwell they had found Billy the Zip. They'd told him they had eliminated him. Maxwell had nodded, grinned and then gone on to other things. He seemed to be embarrassed by the fact that he had ordered a man killed. He didn't try to alibi his way out of it. He ignored it, making a single note in a file and putting the file into his desk drawer.

"You don't want to hear about it?" Fetterman asked. As always, he was leaning against the filing cabinets.

"I've got all the information I need."

"What about his POW camp?" Gerber asked.

"No."

"We wiped out the camp," said Gerber. "Burned it and left the bodies where they fell."

"Fine," said Maxwell. "I'll report that through channels, as well."

"What about the women?" Gerber asked.

"What women?"

"The ones we told you about in Dong Xoai. The ones the ARVN were harassing."

"I don't know anything about those women. I haven't had time to check on them."

"Great," said Gerber. "We ask for one favor and all we get is nothing from you. So I've got another question. You told us there was a reward for Billy the Zip. How do we apply for it?"

"You're kidding," said Maxwell.

"Nope," said Fetterman. "We earned it and I think we should get it."

"The body," said Maxwell. "You left the body out there."

"But I have his revolver," said Fetterman.

"You aren't actually going to try to collect the reward, are you?" asked Maxwell.

Gerber took a deep breath. "I suppose it would be months before the ARVN would pay up, and then the IRS would be standing there with their hand out."

"Not for me," said Fetterman. "My income is not taxable while I'm in Vietnam."

Maxwell shook his head. "If the comedy routine is finished..."

As they started to leave, Fetterman pulled up his jungle jacket and took out the six-shooter. He moved forward, set it on Maxwell's desk and said, "See that it gets back to the rightful owner."

Maxwell didn't say a word. He knew exactly where the revolver had come from.

They left then, unhappy with Maxwell's attitude. They'd done what he'd asked, eliminated Billy the Zip, and now he was treating them as if they'd done something wrong. Maybe if there had been a couple of POWs to free, everyone would be patting them on the back and handing out sackfuls of medals.

They went off to eat dinner with Robin Morrow. She had a ton of questions for them, wanting to know whether they had discovered anything about the NVA soldier who thought he was Billy the Kid.

Gerber shrugged as if he didn't know what she was talking about, but that didn't work. She'd heard the rumors and she'd learned a few things that had helped them.

"Don't try that dumb routine on me this time," she told him.

So Gerber said they had gone in search of the Vietnamese version of Billy the Kid but hadn't found him. Her stories in the papers had produced no response. It had been a long shot at best.

Grinning, she said, "Well, at least Tony has the reputation as the fastest gun in the East."

But, as they ate, she pushed a little more, even though she knew there wasn't much they could, or would, tell her. Finally she gave up and let the whole thing go.

But the thing that had bothered both Gerber and Fetterman was the ARVN and the two women at the road side stand. Gerber believed that their chasing the ARVN away might have put them in jeopardy.

It had taken no time to arrange a chopper flight. Both were dressed in clean jungle fatigues and both carried their M-16s. Under his fatigue jacket Gerber carried his Browning M-35 pistol. Fetterman wore the gun belt he'd taken from Billy the Zip, along with the revolver he'd pried from the Vietnamese gunfighter's fingers.

Now they were sitting on the porch of the roadhouse. All was as it had been. Drinking the last of his Coke, Fetterman said, "It's about time for the chopper to return."

Gerber tipped his chair back and nodded, trying to think of something to say. He drank some of the Coke.

"Shit," said Fetterman suddenly. "There's an ARVN truck coming up the road."

"Déjà vu," said Gerber. He rocked forward, the front legs of the chair thudding on the floor. "It can't be the same guys."

The truck slowed and stopped at the edge of the road. Eight men climbed out of the rear and two came from the cab. One was an officer. The same officer.

"Maybe he won't recognize us," said Gerber. "We all look the same to them."

The officer walked up onto the porch and stopped. He stared at Fetterman, then at Gerber. Grinning, he said, "I see the smartass has returned."

"We don't want any trouble," said Gerber.

"Then you should never have come back. You killed one of my men. You made me look bad in front of the others. And now I have you outnumbered."

The door banged open, and the old woman started out. She froze when she saw who it was and then retreated hastily. She didn't utter a word.

"You had us outnumbered before," said Gerber. He shifted around so that he could grab his M-16 if he needed it. "Why not just let it lie?"

"Because I looked bad in front of my men," he said. "I have to get even."

Fetterman stood up suddenly, his chair tipping over behind him. He pushed his jungle jacket aside so that the bottom of it was behind the revolver. It was a gesture he'd seen cowboys do on TV and in movies a hundred times. He was getting ready to draw. He said nothing.

The ARVN officer watched with interest at first. Then he saw the holster and revolver and he knew what had happened. He knew Fetterman had been the man who had killed Van. The rumors had been circulating ever since the gunfight. A fair fight where an American had outdrawn and killed the fastest Vietnamese.

"We are allies," said the officer. "We should not be confronting each other this way."

"True enough," said Gerber. "We should be helping one another."

"Exactly," said the ARVN officer.

Gerber pointed at the door and raised his voice. "Please bring enough Cokes for my new friends." He glanced at the officer. "A treat on me."

"Of course. Thank you."

Fetterman relaxed then. He sat down and picked up his Coke.

The ARVN officer joined them. He stared at Fetterman. "Are you really that fast?"

"Faster," said Gerber. "You wouldn't have stood a chance with him."

At that moment the helicopter reappeared. It came down slowly and landed on the road near the ARVN truck. Gerber drained his Coke, stood and picked up his M-16. "That's our ride." He pulled several MPC bills from his pocket and dropped them onto the table. "To your health."

"Thank you, Dai Uy," said the Vietnamese.

Together Fetterman and Gerber left the porch and walked toward the chopper. Fetterman patted the butt of the revolver. "A reputation isn't always a bad thing."

Gerber nodded. "Sometimes it's the only thing."

"Yes, sir. Sometimes."

GLOSSARY

AC—Aircraft Commander. The pilot in charge of the aircraft.

ADO—A-Detachment's area of operations.

AFVN—Armed Forces radio and television network in Vietnam. Army PFC Pat Sajak was probably the most memorable of AFVN's DJs with his loud and long, "GOOOOOOOOOOOOOD MORNing, Vietnam!" Mr. Sajak now seeks his fortune on late-night television.

AGGRESSOR FATIGUES—Black fatigues called aggressor fatigues because they are the color of the uniforms worn by aggressors during war games in the World during training.

AIT—Advanced Individual Training. The school soldiers are sent to after basic training.

AK-47—Assault rifle normally used by the North Vietnamese and Vietcong.

ANGRY-109—AN-109, the radio used by the Special Forces for long-range communications.

AN/PRR9 and AN/PRT4—Intrasquad radio receiver and transmitter used for short-range communications. The range is something under a mile.

AO—Area of Operations.

AO DAI—Long dresslike garment, split up the sides and worn over pants.

AP—Air Police. The old designation for the guards on air force bases. Now referred to as security police.

AP ROUNDS—Armor-piercing ammunition.

APU—Auxiliary Power Unit. An outside source of power used to start aircraft engines.

ARC LIGHT—Term used for a B-52 bombing mission. Also known as heavy arty.

ARVN—Army of the Republic of Vietnam. A South Vietnamese soldier. Also known as Marvin Arvin.

ASA—Army Security Agency.

ASH AND TRASH—Refers to helicopter support missions that didn't involve a direct combat role. They hauled supplies, equipment, mail and all sorts of ash and trash.

AST—Control officer between the men in isolation and the outside world. He is responsible for taking care of all problems.

AUTOVON—Army phone system that allows soldiers on one base to call another base, bypassing the civilian phone system.

BDA—Bomb Damage Assessment. The official report on how well a bombing mission went.

BIG RED ONE—Nickname of the First Infantry Division, derived from the big red numeral 1 on the shoulder patch.

BISCUIT—C-rations.

BODY COUNT—Number of enemy killed, wounded or captured during an operation. Used by Saigon and Washington as a means of measuring the progress of the war.

BOOM BOOM—Term used by Vietnamese prostitutes to sell their product.

BOONDOGGLE—Any military operation that hasn't been completely thought out. An operation that is ridiculous.

BOONIE HATS—Soft cap worn by a grunt in the field when not wearing his steel pot.

BROWNING M-2—Fifty-caliber machine gun manufactured by Browning.

BROWNING M-35—A 9 mm automatic pistol that became the favorite of the Special Forces.

BUSHMASTER—Jungle warfare expert or soldier skilled in jungle navigation. Also a large deadly snake not common to Vietnam but mighty tasty.

C AND C—Command and Control aircraft that circled overhead to direct combined air and ground operations.

CAO BOI—Cowboy. A term that referred to the criminals of Saigon who rode motorcycles.

CARIBOU—Cargo Transport plane.

CHECKRIDE—Flight in which one pilot checks the proficiency of another. It can be an informal review of the various techniques or a very formal test of a pilot's knowledge.

CHINOOK—Army Aviation twin-engine helicopter. A CH-47. Also known as a shit hook.

CHOCK—Refers to the number of the aircraft in the flight. Chock Three is the third, Chock Six the sixth.

CLAYMORE—Antipersonnel mine that fires seven hundred and fifty steel balls with a lethal range of fifty meters.

CLOSE AIR SUPPORT—Use of airplanes and helicopters to fire on enemy units near friendlies.

CO CONG—Female Vietcong.

COLT—Soviet-built small transport plane. The NATO code name for Soviet and Warsaw Pact transports all begin with the letter *C*.

CONEX—Steel container about ten feet high, ten feet deep and ten feet long used to haul equipment and supplies.

CS—Refers to a chemical similar to tear gas used in Vietnam. Actually it was a fine powder that could lie dormant for weeks until stirred up by men walking through it or by the rotor wash of landing helicopters.

DAC CONG—Enemy sappers who attacked in the front ranks to blow up the wire so that the infantry could assault a camp.

DAI UY—Vietnamese army rank equivalent to captain.

DEROS—Date Estimated Return from Overseas Service.

DIRNSA—Director, National Security Agency.

E AND E—Escape and Evasion.

FEET WET—Term used by pilots to describe a flight over water.

FIELD GRADE—Refers to officers above the rank of captain and below that of brigadier general. In other words, majors, lieutenant colonels and colonels.

FIRECRACKER—Special artillery shell that explodes into a number of small bomblets that detonate later. An artillery version of the cluster bomb, it was employed as a secret weapon tactically for the first time at Khe Sanh.

FIREFLY—Helicopter with a battery of bright lights mounted in it or on it. The aircraft was designed to draw enemy fire at night so that gunships orbiting close by could attack the target.

FIRST SHIRT—Military term referring to the first sergeant.

FIVE—Radio call sign for the executive officer of a unit.

FOB—Forward Operating Base.

FOX MIKE—FM radio.

FNG—Fucking New Guy.

FREEDOM BIRD—Name given to any aircraft that took troops out of Vietnam. Usually referred to the commercial jet flights that took men back to the World.

GARAND—M-1 rifle that was replaced by the M-14. Issued to the South Vietnamese early in the war.

GO-TO-HELL-RAG—Towel or any large cloth worn around the neck by a grunt.

GRAIL—NATO name for shoulder-fired SA-7 surface-to-air missile.

GUARD THE RADIO—Term that means standing by in the commo bunker and listening for messages.

GUIDELINE—NATO name for SA-2 surface-to-air missile.

GUNSHIP—Armed Helicopter or cargo plane that carries weapons instead of cargo.

HE—High Explosive ammunition.

HOOTCH—Almost any shelter, from temporary to long-term.

HORN—Term that referred to a specific kind of radio operations that used satellites to rebroadcast messages.

HORSE—See *Biscuit*.

HOTEL THREE—Helicopter landing area at Saigon's Tan Son Nhut Airport.

HUEY—UH-1 helicopter.

HUMINT—Human intelligence resource.

ICS—Official name of the intercom system in an aircraft.

IN-COUNTRY—Term used to refer to American troops operating in South Vietnam. They were all in-country.

INTELLIGENCE—Any information about enemy operations. It can include troop movements, weapons capabilities, biographies of enemy commanders and general information about terrain features. It is any information that would be useful in planning a mission.

KA-BAR—Type of military combat knife.

KIA—Killed In Action. (Since the U.S. wasn't engaged in a declared war, the use of the term KIA wasn't authorized. KIA came to mean enemy dead. Americans were KHA, or Killed in Hostile Action.)

KLICK—A thousand meters. A kilometer.

LIMA LIMA—Land Line. Refers to telephone communications between two points on the ground.

LLDB—Luc Luong Dac Biet. The South Vietnamese Special Forces. Sometimes referred to as the Look Long, Duck Back.

LOW QUARTERS—Military term for regular shoes. In the case of the Army, it means the black dress shoes worn with the Class A and Dress uniforms.

LP—Listening Post. A position outside the perimeter manned by a couple of people to give advance warning of enemy activity.

LRRP—Long Range Reconnaissance Patrol.

LSA—Lubricant used by soldiers on their weapons to ensure they would continue to operate properly.

LZ—Landing Zone.

M-3—Also known as a grease gun. A .45-caliber submachine gun favored in World War II by GIs. Its slow rate of fire meant the barrel didn't rise. As well, the user didn't burn through his ammo as fast as he did with some of his other weapons.

M-14—Standard rifle of the U.S., eventually replaced by the M-16. It fires the standard NATO round— 7.62 mm.

M-16—Became the standard infantry weapon of the Vietnam War. It fires 5.56 mm ammunition.

M-79—Short-barreled, shoulder-fired weapon that fires a 40 mm grenade. These can be high explosives, white phosphorus or canister.

M-113—Numerical designation of an armored personnel carrier.

MACV—Military Assistance Command, Vietnam, replaced MAAG in 1964.

MAD MINUTE—Specified time in a base camp when the men in the bunkers would clear their weapons. It came to mean the random firing of all the camp's weapons just as fast as everyone could shoot.

MATCU—Marine Air Traffic Control Unit.

MEDEVAC—Also called Dust-off. A helicopter used to take wounded to medical facilities.

MI—Military Intelligence.

MIA—Missing In Action.

MONOPOLY MONEY—Term used by the servicemen in Vietnam to describe the MPC handed out in lieu of regular U.S. currency.

MOS—Military Occupation Specialty. A job description.

MPC—Military Payment Certificates. Used by military in lieu of U.S. dollars.

NCO—Noncommissioned officer. A noncom. A sergeant.

NCOIC—NCO In Charge. The senior NCO in a unit, detachment or patrol.

NDB—Nondirectional beacon. A radio beacon that can be used for homing.

NEXT—The man who said it was his turn next to be rotated home. See *Short*.

NINETEEN—Average age of combat soldier in Vietnam, as opposed to twenty-six in World War II.

NVA—North Vietnamese Army. Also used to designate a soldier from North Vietnam.

ONTOS—Marine weapon that consists of six 106 mm recoilless rifles mounted on a tracked vehicle.

ORDER OF BATTLE—A listing of the units available during a battle.

P (PIASTER)—Basic monetary unit in South Vietnam worth slightly less than a penny.

PETA-PRIME—Tarlike substance that melted in the heat of the day to become a sticky black nightmare that clung to boots, clothes and equipment. It was used to hold down the dust during the dry season.

PETER PILOT—Copilot in a helicopter.

PLF—Parachute Landing Fall. The roll used by parachutists on landing.

POL—Petroleum, Oil and Lubricants. The refueling point on many military bases.

POW—Prisoner of war.

PRC-10—Portable radio.

PRC-25—Lighter portable radio that replaced the PRC-10.

PULL PITCH—Term used by helicopter pilots that means they are going to take off.

PUNJI STAKE—Sharpened bamboo hidden to penetrate the foot. Sometimes dipped in feces.

PUZZLE PALACE—Term referring to the Pentagon. It was called the puzzle palace because no one knew what was going on in it. The Puzzle Palace East referred to MACV or USARV Headquarters in Saigon.

REDLEGS—Term that refers to artillerymen. It derives from the old Army where artillerymen wore red stripes on the legs of their uniforms.

REMF—Rear Echelon Motherfucker.

RINGKNOCKER—Graduate of a military academy. Refers to the ring worn by all graduates.

RLO—Real Live Officer. A term used by warrant officers in reference to commissioned officers.

RON—Remain Overnight. Term used by flight crews to indicate a flight that would last longer than a day.

RPD—Soviet 7.62 mm light machine gun.

RTO—Radio Telephone Operator. The radioman of a unit.

RUFF-PUFFS—Term applied to RF-PFs, the regional and popular forces. Militia drawn from local population.

S-3—Company-level operations officer. The same as the G-3 on a general's staff.

SA-2—Surface-to-air missile fired from a fixed site. A radar-guided missile nearly thirty-five feet long.

SA-7—Surface-to-air missile that is shoulder-fired and has infrared homing.

SACSA—Special Assistant for Counterinsurgency and Special Activities.

SAFE AREA—Selected Area For Evasion. It doesn't mean the area is safe from the enemy, only that the terrain, location or local population make the area a good place for escape and evasion.

SAM TWO—Refers to the SA-2 Guideline.

SAR—Search and Rescue. SAR forces were the people involved in search-and-rescue missions.

SECDEF—Secretary of Defense.

SHORT-TIME—GI term for a quickie.

SHORT-TIMER—Person who had been in Vietnam for nearly a year and who would be rotated back to the World soon. When the DEROS (Date of Estimated Return from Overseas Services) was the shortest in the unit, the person was said to be next.

SINGLE-DIGIT MIDGET—Soldier with fewer than ten days left in-country.

SIX—Radio call sign for unit commander.

SKATE—Term similar to goldbricking. It meant goofing off when there was work to be done.

SKS—Soviet-made carbine.

SOI—Signal Operating Instructions. The booklet that contained the call signs and radio frequencies of the units in Vietnam.

SOP—Standard Operating Procedure.

SPIKE TEAM—Special Forces team made up for a direct-action mission.

STEEL POT—Standard U.S. Army helmet. The steel pot was the outer metal cover.

TAOR—Tactical Area of Operational Responsibility.

TEAM UNIFORM OR COMPANY UNIFORM—UHF radio frequency on which the team or the company communicates. Frequencies were changed periodically in an attempt to confuse the enemy.

THE WORLD—The United States.

THREE—Radio call sign of the operations officer.

THREE CORPS—Military area around Saigon. Vietnam was divided into four corps areas.

TO&E—Table of Organization and Equipment. A detailed listing of all men and equipment assigned to a unit.

TOC—Tactical Operations Center.

TOT—Time Over Target. Refers to the time that the aircraft is supposed to be over the drop zone with the parachutists, or the target if the plane is a bomber.

TRICK CHIEF—NCOIC for a shift.

TRIPLE A—Antiaircraft Artillery or AAA. Anything used to shoot at airplanes and helicopters.

TWO—Radio call sign of the intelligence officer.

TWO-OH-ONE (201) FILE—Military records file that listed all of a soldier's qualifications, training, experience and abilities. It was passed from unit to unit so that the new commander would have some idea about the capabilities of an incoming soldier.

UMZ—Ultramilitarized Zone. The name GIs gave to the DMZ (Demilitarized Zone).

UNIFORM—Refers to the UHF radio. Company Uniform would be the frequency assigned to that company.

USARV—United States Army, Vietnam.

VC—Vietcong, called Victor Charlie (Phonetic alphabet) or just Charlie.

VIETCONG—Contraction of Vietnam Cong San (Vietnamese Communist).

VIETCONG SAN—Vietnamese Communists. A term in use since 1956.

WHITE MICE—Referred to the South Vietnamese military police because they all wore white helmets.

WIA—Wounded In Action.

WILLIE PETE—WP, white phosphorus, called smoke rounds. Also used as antipersonnel weapons.

WOBBLY ONE—Refers to a W-1, the lowest warrant officer grade. Helicopter pilots who weren't commissioned started out as Wobbly Ones.

WSO—Weapons Systems Officer. The name given to the man who rode in the back seat of a Phantom because he was responsible for the weapons systems.

XM-21—Name given to the Army's sniper rifle. An M-14 with a special ART scope.

XO—Executive officer of a unit.

X RAY—Term that refers to an engineer assigned to a unit.

ZAP—To ding, pop caps or shoot. To kill.

Introducing Max Horn. He's not your typical cop. But then, nothing's typical in the year 2025.

HORN

HOT ZONE

BEN SLOANE

The brutal attack left New York Police Detective Max Horn clinging to life and vowing to seek vengeance on the manic specter who murdered his wife and young son. Now, thanks to cold hard cash and the genius of an underground techno-doc, Max is a new man with a few new advantages—titanium skin and biomechanical limbs hard-wired to his central nervous system.

On an asteroid called New Pittsburgh, Max walks a new beat...and in a horrible twist of fate comes face-to-face with the man who killed his family.

Look for HORN #1—HOT ZONE in March wherever paperbacks are sold because once you meet Max Horn, you'll never forget him.

DON PENDLETON'S
THE EXECUTIONER®
FEATURING MACK BOLAN

Baptized in the fire and blood of Vietnam, Mack Bolan has become America's supreme hero. Fiercely patriotic and compassionate, he's a man with a high moral code whose sense of right and wrong sometimes violates society's rules. In adventures filled with heart-stopping action, Bolan has thrilled readers around the world. Experience the high-voltage charge as Bolan rallies to the call of his own conscience in daring exploits that place him in peril with virtually every heartbeat.

"Anyone who stands against the civilized forces of truth and justice will sooner or later have to face the piercing blue eyes and cold Beretta steel of Mack Bolan . . . civilization's avenging angel."
—*San Francisco Examiner*

Available wherever paperbacks are sold.

MB-2RR

Illegal nuclear testing in Antarctica sends Phoenix Force Down Under when a maniacal plot threatens global destruction.

=== SUPER PHOENIX FORCE #3 ===

COLD DEAD

GAR WILSON

The two superpowers suspect one another of illegal nuclear testing in Antarctica when the bodies of two murdered scientists show high levels of radiation in their systems.

It's a crisis situation that leads Phoenix Force to New Zealand, where a madman's growing arsenal of nuclear weapons is destined for sale on the international black market....

Don't miss the riveting confrontation in COLD DEAD when it explodes onto the shelves at your favorite retail outlet in April, or reserve your copy for March shipping by sending your name, address, zip or postal code along with a check or money order for $4.70 (includes 75¢ postage and handling) payable to Gold Eagle Books:

In the U.S.
901 Fuhrmann Blvd.
Box 1325
Buffalo, NY 14269-1325

In Canada
P.O. Box 609
Fort Erie, Ontario
L2A 5X3

GOLD EAGLE®

Please specify book title with your order.

SPF3-1

ABLE TEAM®

DICK STIVERS

Action writhes in the reader's own streets as Able Team's Carl "Ironman" Lyons, Pol Blancanales and Gadgets Schwarz make triple trouble in blazing war. Join Dick Stivers's Able Team—the country's finest tactical neutralization squad in an era of urban terror and unbridled crime.

"Able Team will go anywhere, do anything, in order to complete their mission. Plenty of action! Recommended!"
—*West Coast Review of Books*

Able Team titles are available wherever paperbacks are sold.

GOLD EAGLE®

AT-1R-A